# Damaged
# Beyond
# Repair

## ALISHA YVONNE

# Damaged Beyond Repair

## ALISHA YVONNE

UpWrite Creations Press
Cordova, TN 38018

ISBN 10: 1-73749-730-1
ISBN 13: 978-1-7374973-0-1
Library of Congress Number 2021913423

First Printing: July 2021

Printed in the United States of America

10 9 8 7 6 5 4 3 2 1

*This is a work of fiction. Any references or similarities to actual events, real people, living, or dead, or to real locals are intended to give the novel a sense of reality. Any similarity in other names, characters, places, and incidents is entirely coincidental.*

## For

Tonia

# Sydney

## 1

My best friend, Roxie, was all over him. Howard F. Bland III—a smooth, even-toned caramel, six-foot-two, businessman—who also happened to be my husband. In the eighteen months of knowing Roxie, I never imagined she would become such a flirt—and with my husband at that. But she had.

There was no denying it. Roxie Mills was arguably the most stunning woman in the room. Statuesque, her 5'9 frame commanded attention as she sashayed across the venue in her soft cinnamon-hue, low-back, spaghetti-strapped gown. Its color and satin fabric accented her bronzed skin tone in a queenly manner. Though very fitted, the dress featured a high-cut split at the leg which aided in her effortless movement.

I was just a tad bit jealous of my friend, but couldn't help it. After trying, unsuccessfully, to lose weight for two years, I still had the stomach pouch that came after the birth of Hailey, the only child Howard and I were able to have. True, Roxie was newly single and had no children, but she and I were both forty, so she should have packed on more weight by now—at least that was how I felt.

Roxie's ex-husband, Calvin, left her for another man. She was devastated, but she was also glad Calvin's secret was discovered only months into what he called his "experimental" affair. Calvin insisted he wasn't gay, but according to Roxie, he never could explain why he moved in with his trial lover shortly after Roxie kicked him out. Still, none of this was reason enough for her to be all over Howard. I was puzzled by her behavior.

It was a big night for Howard. Champion Network Marketing, his employer, held an awards banquet that honored their top affiliate marketers at the elite Madison Hotel. Roxie was invited because Howard had a few extra dinner passes. I felt my husband was a deserving man, and I wanted him to have all the support in the world. Though I called everyone I knew to join the celebration, Roxie was the only one who could make it. The rest of Howard's family lived in various parts of Tennessee, hours from Memphis, which made it difficult to take off work and show up on such short notice. I was actually happy that Roxie decided to come, but shortly after she arrived, I second-guessed having offered the invitation.

Considering the way Roxie carried on, Howard's colleagues would've surely thought Roxie was his wife had I not been in their company many times over the eight years of his employment. What sickened me even more was the fact that Howard let her cling to him. I wondered what others might've been thinking as they posed for pictures. I asked Roxie to step out of the way on several occasions.

"One more shot," Kevin Johnson, Howard's longtime friend and coworker said, peering through his camera.

Kevin was one of the newest members of Champion Network Marketing—not bad-looking either. Howard helped him land an interview there nearly a year before. His wife, Melanie, and I had become acquainted and loved shopping together as we had similar tastes. Too bad she wasn't feeling well and had to miss the event. However, Kevin seemed to be enjoying himself anyway.

"This time, I want to see more teeth, Howard," Kevin said, teasing. "Did you not just receive the bonus and award for Best Affiliate Marketer? That's enough reason to grin from ear-to-ear right there, my man!"

Everyone laughed. Roxie leaned her head on Howard's shoulder and placed her hand on his chest as I stood on his other side. Howard wrapped his arm around my lower back, pulling me closer.

"Damn, Howard, you look like a playah, bro," Kevin said as he snapped the picture.

"Um, Kevin," I called, pointing. "Will you grab our camera on the table over there? I'd like you to snap one more picture." I turned to Roxie. "Roxie, do me a favor and sit this one out. I'd like one of just me and Howard this time."

"Oh, sure," Roxie said with no hesitation.

*That was easy*, I thought. *Too easy, considering how she'd huffed and rolled her eyes the other times I asked her to step out of the way.* Kevin figured out how to focus the shot with our new Nikon camera and then took three shots of me leaning on the man of the hour. Just when I was about to thank Kevin, Roxie jumped back onto Howard's arm.

"Okay, that's enough of the love birds," Roxie said. "Let me back into the pictures. Here . . . use my iPhone." She fumbled through her handbag. "I didn't get all dressed up for nothing."

Howard and Kevin looked at me simultaneously. I'm sure they noticed the enthusiasm leave my flesh like a separate entity casting itself out. I couldn't have mustered a smile even if I had wanted one. Roxie gave Kevin her phone. He fidgeted with it, seemingly not knowing what to do next. After several seconds of silence, he spoke up.

"Um, what's up, Sydney?" Kevin asked. "You down? You seem kinda tired to me."

"Yeah, I am," I answered, walking toward him. My eyes slowly scanned Kevin's entire six-foot frame—from the bottom up—until I stared square into his eyes. "I'm done. We've got more than enough pictures for the night." My lips were tight.

I turned back to our table and sat. I figured that was Howard's cue to have a seat with me, but when I looked up, he hadn't moved and Roxie leaned in to whisper something in his ear. *How dare she?* I thought. Howard nodded once, and then they posed for one click of the camera on her iPhone. I stared at Howard, desperately wanting to give him the evil eye, but Stephanie, one of his colleagues walked over to congratulate him before he could make it back to our table.

"What's up, big money?" she said.

"Oh, y'all need to stop that," Howard responded. "The check looks good, but it's not like it's taking me into     another tax bracket, ya know." He chuckled.

"At least not yet, but you're well on your way," she told him.

Howard glanced at me then beckoned me into the conversation. I headed their way, and then decided I wanted Kevin to get a shot of the three of us. I was too late. Kevin was heading in different direction, chatting with another Champion staff member. I thought perhaps Roxie wouldn't mind taking the picture for us, but after combing the room for her, I spied her heading toward a hallway. This was my first time at this particular venue, so I could only presume the hallway led to the restrooms. Stephanie continued to tease as I approached.

"Mrs. Big Money," she called. "How are you?"

I politely smiled and reached to shake her hand.

Stephanie was a lean, average height, butter-complexion woman with long, dark hair and model-like features.

"I'm good, Stephanie. How are you?" she answered.

"I'm fine, but I'd be doing a whole lot better if I had just a fraction of the bonus your husband just got. So, what are the big plans, if I'm not being too nosey?" She glanced back and forth between us.

"Well, this is the first time Howard has gotten this honor, so I'm not sure how much it is. Besides, he's the one who earned it, so I'm fine with whatever he decides to do with it."

"Aw, aren't you the perfect little wife," she said, winking. "I hope you know what you got, Howard, 'cuz had it been me, you would've opened that envelope right here and now!"

We giggled, but Howard gave a short-lived chuckle. He seemed preoccupied as he glanced around the room. "Yeah, well, I think I'm going to surprise my wife." He rubbed my back. "My baby deserves an island vacation, so wherever she wants to go, we'll be there this summer."

Stephanie gasped. "Summer is around the corner."

"I know," Howard stated. "The sooner the better. You know Hailey just hit the terrible two stage, so Sydney could use a break."

"Are you serious? Hailey's two already?" Stephanie asked.

I nodded. "Time is flying, huh?"

Stephanie grabbed my hand. "Girl, before you know it, she'll be in kindergarten. Can you imagine?"

As I shook my head, Howard released his embrace. "Excuse me, ladies," he said, leaving us standing.

I couldn't believe how he abruptly left. I wanted to ask where he was going, but he was gone quicker than I could get my thoughts together. My eyes trailed him, but Stephanie distracted me as she rambled. She held her hand out so I could see her engagement ring. It was flawless. I took my eyes off Howard for a moment—long enough to study the platinum, three-carat, princess-cut beauty.

"Oh gosh, Stephanie." I pulled her hand closer to my eyes. "This is gorgeous. I've never even met your beau. You've never brought him to any of the company's functions. Who is this masked man?"

She cleared her throat. "Well, no, I haven't. I had to make sure he was the right one for me before bringing him around family and friends. We've been together for nearly two years now, and he just sprung the question Fourth of July weekend. I accepted, but I sort of felt bad that I got engaged before my parents had a chance to meet him."

I briefly scanned the room for Howard. He was nowhere to be found. "Oh, I hope your family understood your reasons," I responded, my mind really going elsewhere.

"My father wasn't thrilled, but once we all sat down and talked over dinner, he got to know my fiancé a bit."

"That's great, Stephanie. Listen . . . will you excuse me? I need to step out for a moment."

"Sure, Sydney. I'll see you when you get back."

Stephanie and I pivoted in opposite directions. My mind was totally gone. I needed to find my husband. I had a notion to head where I'd seen Roxie go. Once into the hall, I discovered there was a nearby ladies' room. My heart ached as it pounded against my chest. I slowly approached the door, fighting conflicting thoughts. This felt like a setup—setting myself up to be hurt. But I also yearned to know if my instincts were right. Howard and Roxie had been acting strange all night, and then they happened to be missing at the same time.

I eased the restroom door opened. Soft cries of pleasure disappointed my ears and punctured my heart as I slowly crept inside. I recognized the voice to be that of Roxie's. After gently closing the door, I took off my heels to muffle my footsteps. Roxie seemed totally comfortable with what she was doing. She continued her sexual talk and sensual moans.

"Damn, baby, I love this," she crooned. "Oh, hell yeah. You need to get a bonus more often . . . or do whatever's got you happy, 'cuz you workin' me, baby."

My heart sank. I could hear his raspy pants. Warm tears nearly blinded me as I desperately shook off the hurt. *Un-un . . . don't you do it,* I told myself. *Don't you dare cry . . . you confront their cheating asses and send them on the fast track to hell!*

I started toward the stall and then abruptly stopped. My breathing grew louder and rougher. Tears came in spite me trying to toughen up. Then, they heard my sniffles.

"Somebody's out there," one of them whispered. "Peek and see who it is."

"No. You peek," the other voice whispered.

"Shhh. Be quiet."

Anger set in. I stopped crying and wiped the tears from my cheeks. My chest heaved, and I could no longer breathe through my nostrils. Visions of me murdering them flashed across my mind. But then I remembered I brought a different purse. I had an urge for my nine-millimeter like a lioness wanting prey.

# Roxie

## 2

I know I heard someone in the restroom with us, but I was too afraid to look. We kept silent until we were confident no one was out there. The heat between my legs pulsated during our brief pause. I wanted him driving his hardness deep inside of me as he had only moments before. We faced each other. He held one of my legs over his arm and cupped his other hand under my bottom. I initiated things all over again. I began to grind, hoping to remind him why we were there, and that intermission was *over*. The play was back in session without a proper warning. I squealed as he caught me off guard with the first thrust.

"Ooooooo, baby, damn!" I moaned.

"Sssshhh. Are you trying to get us caught," he said in a whisper so low, I barely understood him. "Sydney could come in here looking for you."

I shook my head then whispered, "Oh, you're worried about her? Get off me." When he didn't immediately move, I yelled. "Now!"

He didn't release me. Instead, he raised my leg to his shoulder then gripped my ass with both hands as he drove long, hard strokes into me. I couldn't remember the last time I took such length. He was good—damned good—no he was great—and he took me to my favorite place. Ecstasy. I trembled as I released a long-winded sigh that I couldn't soften if I tried. He cupped my mouth then buried his head into my neck, muffling his moan as he released also.

"Damn," he said, panting as he slowly lifted his head to look at me. "I think we almost got caught. You know that, right?"

"Well, don't feel too confident now, mister. We've still got to sneak out of here before anyone sees us."

"Damn. True. Got any suggestions?"

He eased my leg off of him then pulled up his pants.

"Ew, that's nasty," I said. "Don't you want some wet paper towels or something to clean up first?"

He chuckled. "Naw. I want to go home and remember your scent."

"Ugh. Okay. Whatever. I'm going to the sink."

"Wait," he said. "How am I going to get out of here without being caught?"

I shrugged. "How did you get in here without being seen?" I exited the stall. "Wait until after you've heard me leave."

I cleaned up at the sink. *I did it,* I thought. *I've wanted him for so long, and tonight it finally happened.* Once finished, I turned off the water then bid him goodnight.

"It was fun. We'll have to do it again some time," I said over my shoulder.

"Sure," I heard him say as I exited the restroom.

The engagement was still in session as I expected. All was as I remembered before I entered the restroom—all except one thing—Sydney! Her eyes were fixed on me as I stood in the entryway that led to the restrooms. She seemed bothered. Her body was stiff, and her eyes focused on me, unblinkingly. She made me nervous. I couldn't read her. I didn't know if her disposition was one of anger, shock, or pain. Either way, I could see she clearly wasn't happy.

I started toward her. I couldn't let her see him come from the direction of the restrooms. Our friendship would be totally compromised, and his life would never be the same. Her chest heaved as I stepped closer.

"What's up, girl?" I sang in a mild tone. She didn't answer. "Syd," I said and tried to pull her arm. She was stiffer than I knew. "Are you okay? You seem upset. Did something happen while I was in the restroom?"

She finally shifted her posture, but it was a stance that almost made me want to run. Sydney stood with one foot in front of the other, clinching tight fists at her sides. I stuttered my next words.

"Um, um, Syd, look. Clearly, s-s-something has happened to upset you. W-w-where's Howard?"

Her nose hardened. "You tell me," she demanded.

"I don't know. Sydney, what's wrong?"

"Sydney," a feminine voice called. "Sydney," the woman called again as she approached us.

Sydney kept her eyes fixed on me. I wanted to turn and look toward the restrooms, but I dared not.

"Sydney, come outside for a moment. I want you to meet my fiancé. I didn't think he was

15

going to make it, but he's here, and *Howard* just stepped outside from nowhere, cracking all sorts of marital jokes." The tall, lean woman giggled.

Sydney's head snapped. Her interest seemed to be piqued by the sound of Howard's name.

"Girl, you've got to come join us. They're double-teaming me," the thin woman continued.

The woman pulled Sydney's arm. Her body relaxed enough to allow the woman to lead her outside.

"Sorry," the woman yelled over her shoulder to me. "She'll be back shortly."

I watched them leave the ballroom and head into the hallway. My nerves were shot. I could only assume that somehow Sydney knew about the tryst in the restroom. I knew I heard someone in there. It had to be her. *But why didn't she say anything?* I wondered. She could've busted us, and there wouldn't have been anything either of us could do about it. As I tried to collect my thoughts on  how to deal with Syd, a young cocktail waiter walked up, making small talk.

"Hey, beautiful. Would you like something to drink?"

I glanced at the tray in his hands. "Yes, I think I better."

His eyebrows rose. "Whoa. What does that mean?"

"We're not even halfway through the night, and it has already become a long one. So, it's either I leave now or have a tall glass of courage to help me stick it out."

"Wow," the chiseled face, smooth, chocolate man said. "Well, in that case, take a Long Island Tea instead of a wine cooler. Maybe that will help you relax and enjoy yourself."

"Thanks." I reached for the attractive brown mixture, decorated with a slice of lemon and a tiny umbrella.

"This is a nice event your employer has put on," he said.

"Oh, I'm not employed with this company. I'm here with friends."

"Well, where are they? I could've sworn you were here by yourself."

I glanced around the room, and then toward the entrance. "I'm not sure. I think they're just outside this room."

"Well, what kind of friends are they to leave you standing alone? Did they not invite you to join them?" He glanced toward the doorway.

I shook my head. "No, they didn't."

"All things happen for a reason, I guess."

My eyebrows rose. "Oh? And what reason might this be?"

"Think about it: If they hadn't left you standing here alone, you might not have caught my attention, so I could get to know you."

"Get to know me? Oh, is that what you think you're doing?"

He smiled. "Well, not as of yet, but I'm certainly working up to it. What's your name, beautiful?"

"Hmm. I think I like 'beautiful'?" I answered, smiling back.

"Then, Beautiful it is. I'm Nigel." He shook my hand.

"Ah, Latin—dark one."

"Yes. Impressive. How did you know?"

"I've done my research on names. Once upon a time I considered Nigel as a name for the son I never had."

"You have girls?"

"No. I don't have children."

"Really?" He tilted his head. "I'm sensing this story might be a sad one, so I won't ask you to elaborate. I'll just ask if we could chat some other time . . . Is it possible I could have your number?"

I nodded then had a second thought. "Wait. You seem a bit young. How old are you?"

"Twenty-six."

"Are you sure?"

He laughed. "Of course, I'm sure. Not unless my mother and birth certificate are lying."

"Nigel, I'm forty."

His lips spread evenly across a marvelous set of pearly-white teeth. "And your point being?"

"Um . . . well, I guess I don't have a point. Let me take *your* number." I pulled out my cell then began to type his number into the contact log as he recited it.

"So, when can I expect to hear from you?" Nigel was persistent. I liked that in him.

"Soon," I offered.

Just then Kevin walked up, frowning. "What's soon?"

"Oh, Nigel and I were just chatting," I answered. "He was just leaving." I turned to Nigel. "Goodnight. Thanks for the drink."

Nigel dipped his head with one nod. "Goodnight, beautiful."

Kevin watched Nigel walk out of earshot then said, "Ready to rob the cradle, are we?"

"Whatever, Kevin. I thought you were gone."

"You did, huh?" He glanced in Nigel's direction, but I called his attention back to me.

"Okay, so he's a baby compared to me, but we were just talking since it seems none of my friends care to be in my company."

"Speaking of friends: Where is everyone?" Kevin glanced around the room.

"I don't know. Sydney walked off with some superstar-looking chick."

He chuckled. "Um, that would be Stephanie."

"Well, I think they're all in the hall, but Sydney seems to be in a bad mood about something."

"In a bad mood? Let me go see what's going on." He walked away from me.

"Oh, so now you're just going to leave me standing, too?" He glanced over his shoulder briefly but kept walking. "Well, good luck on finding out something," I yelled. "I'm outta here."

I took a long swig of my Long Island Tea then set the glass on a nearby table and headed out of the ballroom. Once in the hall, all eyes were on me. Sydney, Howard, Kevin, and even Stephanie and her fine-ass fiancé—they all stared, and no one bothered to offer me a goodbye. I threw up a farewell hand then strutted out of their sight.

The final look on Sydney's face said she knew, but perhaps she felt it wasn't time to confront me. We would hash it out later, but for now, I would take home the memory of having that stallion of a man deep inside of me. Even the scent of his cologne was etched in my nostrils. This might've been his night, but it was certainly mine, too. I'd meet the consequences head on much later.

# Sydney

## 3

There were no ifs, ands, or buts about it—Howard was going to pay for how he hurt me. What should've been a joyous occasion turned out to be a nightmare. My momma always told me that what's done in the dark soon comes to light, but with Howard, I always felt as if the lights were on. Eight glorious years of marriage with no major problems—why would I ever suspect he had secrets?

I stood in the master bath mirror the next morning after my shower, looking at the bags under my eyes. I couldn't remember the last time I cried so much. I hated what I saw—disheveled hair with slightly graying new-growth at the edges, drooping, dry, vanilla skin, and at least fifteen more pounds than I needed on my frame. Just pure sadness—a broken me.

Howard lay in the bed, sleeping like a baby, seemingly unfazed after our long, heated, late-night argument. I was so glad we decided not to pick up Hailey from my sister's house. Teresa loved having her niece over, so leaving Hailey overnight was never an issue. Our poor baby wouldn't have been able to sleep through the screaming and yelling.

After drying off, I put on my panties and the yellow sundress I brought into the bathroom with me. I loved the way my auburn-colored, natural-textured hair looked against the dress. I moisturized my hair then brushed it back so that it lay wavy, all except the curly ponytail that hung loosely after I put a scrunchie on it. Howard liked my hair pulled back. He loved everything about me—or he used to. I had no idea when all of that changed.

I left Howard sleeping in our room and stood at the kitchen island, trying to decide if I wanted breakfast. I couldn't think straight. Howard and I argued the entire night, and I barely closed my eyes for an hour of sleep. Roxie's moans replayed in my mind like a scratched record. I just wanted to throw that record against the wall and smash it, so I could have a sense of relief.

Howard yelled and screamed at me as though I didn't know what I'd heard. Had I busted him in that restroom while I had the chance, he wouldn't had an argument. Regardless of how he wanted to deny it, I knew in the back of my mind that the awards banquet was an eye-opener and a blessing in disguise.

I walked over to the refrigerator, pulled out the carton of eggs and opened it. There were eight eggs remaining. *Hmph,* I thought. I felt like taking them upstairs and smashing each of them in Howard's face—one for each year we were married under false pretenses—the lie that he loved me and would remain faithful until death do us part. I wondered how long Roxie and Howard had been carrying on their affair. *Could she have been sleeping with him while she was married, too? Oh, no!* I thought. *Her ex-husband was sleeping around!* I panicked. I set the eggs on the counter as I began to hyperventilate. I didn't realize it at first, but Howard walked in while my back was to him.

"Syd, are you okay?"

I spun around, holding my chest. "Howard," I gasped.

"Hold on, baby . . . hold on." He helped me over to the breakfast area, in the corner of our kitchen, and then   eased me into a seat. "Wait just a minute. Let me get a paper bag."

It only took him about fifteen seconds to run over to the kitchen drawer and pop open a brown paper lunch sack. He darted back and handed it to me.

"Breathe, baby," he said. "Breathe."

He knew what to do because he'd seen me hyperventilate while I was in labor. The 911 dispatcher instructed him to give me a paper bag to breathe in until the ambulance got there. Our little Hailey was born shortly after arriving at the hospital.

Once I calmed my breathing, the tears began to flow. This wasn't supposed to happen to me. I married the most loving man on this earth—one who would massage my feet, scratch my scalp, and sponge-bathed me when I had walking pneumonia. Someone so loving wasn't supposed to cheat. He wiped my tears as fast as they fell.

"Sydney, baby, you've got to calm down. You're making yourself sick."

"Howard," I spoke softly.

"Yes, baby?" He kneeled in front of me.

"How long?"

"What?"

"Tell me the truth. How long have you and Roxie been—"

He abruptly jumped up. "Are you serious? You still on this? After we had this argument damned near till daylight? Really?"

"Howard, her ex was cheating, too—she found out he had an affair with a man! I need to know how long, and did you protect yourself because I may need to be tested."

I'd never seen Howard so angry. "I don't believe this shit!"

I stood. "Don't talk to me like that, Howard!"

"Why in the hell would I sleep with Roxie?" he continued as if I hadn't said a word. "And why in the hell would you *want* to believe I slept with her?"

"I don't want to believe it, but Howard I know what I heard in that restroom!"

"You heard *me*?" He pounded his palm against his chest.

"No . . . but I heard her, and she said things that let me know it was you in there with her."

He stepped closer to me. At six-foot-two, he couldn't help looking down on my five-foot-eight frame. I tilted my head upward to look into his eyes. There was no hiding just how angry he was.  His eyes were red, and they were fixed on me with a frightening glare.

"And just what do you think you heard her say, Sydney?"

He made me nervous. I stuttered a bit. "She-she-said, um . . . she said something 'bout you need to get a bonus more often because of how you were making her feel."

He bit his bottom lip, causing the tiny triangle patch of hair to disappear under his top row of teeth.  He had a faint after-five shadow, but his goatee was still just as sexy as it had always been. When he released his bottom lip, surprisingly, his tone was calm.

"Did it not occur to you that Kevin also received an award last night?"  I processed his words as he spoke. "Do you not remember Kevin walking up to receive his certificate and bonus for the Most Advanced New Hire?"

He was right.  Kevin was awarded a bonus, too. I  almost shrunk before his eyes, but something still didn't make sense.

I planted my hands on my hips. "Howard, Kevin is happily married!"

"So am I," he countered, his voice elevated once again. "Or, so I thought!"

"What do you mean or so you thought?"

27

"Sydney, weren't we happy? What is going on with *you* that makes you not trust me anymore?"

He had me there. I couldn't respond. I didn't have an answer. I just stared at him until I could think of something feasible.

"All I know is Kevin doesn't seem like the type who would jeopardize his marriage for one night—"

"And I do?"

Well, there went feasible out the window. I was stumped. I knew what I heard in that restroom. Of all the honorees, only two of them were men, and one of them happened to be my husband. I didn't know what else to say.

"No, Howard," I answered, my tone defeated. "You don't. I'm sorry."

"Sydney, I've been faithful to you. I don't want Roxie or any other woman. I'm married to the love of my life. You hear me?"

The waterworks turned on without my permission. "It's just," I managed, barely audible. "It's just—"

His hands trailed the length of my arms then cupped my hands and pulled me to him. I wrapped my arms around him. Once my head landed in his chest, he rested his hands at the small of my back. "It's just what, Syd? Talk to me, baby."

I sniffled. "It's just that I watched Roxie be all over you last night."

"You're not lying about that. We couldn't catch a break for her. But, baby, don't you think it was the alcohol? I mean, Roxie's never been like that with me before."

I shrugged. "Howard, I know what I heard in that restroom."

He stepped back and grabbed my hands. "Okay, baby, if you say she was with someone, then she was, but just know that it wasn't me."

It took me a moment, but I managed to give him a nod. He kissed my forehead then looked into my eyes.

"So, are we good?" His voice was pleading.

"Yes."

"You sure?"

"Yes, I'm sure."

"Good. That's what I want to hear."

He released my hands then headed to the refrigerator. He opened the door and leaned in.

"Whew, I'm starving. So, baby, am I cooking us breakfast, or are you gonna do it?"

My heart still wasn't at ease, but I had to pretend to be—long enough to get the answers I wanted. He rose and peeped around the refrigerator door at me.

"Huh, baby? You want me to cook?"

I didn't respond immediately. My eyes traced the length of him, dressed in his white wifebeater shirt and dark gray pajama bottoms.

"No, why don't you go get dressed before Teresa brings Hailey home. I'll cook."

He closed the refrigerator then walked over to me. "Okay, baby." He cupped the back of my head then pulled my forehead in for a soft kiss. "Baby, I hate Teresa had to miss the fun last night, but I'm also glad she was there to babysit for us."

"Yeah, me, too," I answered dryly.

"I mean, she didn't have a babysitter either, so she might as well have kept the kiddo for us, right?"

"Right."

He stepped back and looked at me. "You a'ight?"

I nodded. "Yeah."

"Syd, are you sure?"

"Yes, Howard. I'm sure."

He kissed my forehead one last time and then my lips. "Good," he said then walked off. "Hey, let's take the baby to see that new Disney movie," he yelled from the living room.

"That'll be fine," I said softly.

"What?"

"I said fine," I responded, this time a little louder.

"Cool. She'll like that. You know she loves all of those kiddie movies—" his voice trailed as he obviously headed up the stairs.

I shook my head, thinking of how the previous night brought about a change in the way I felt toward my husband. I wanted to see him in the manner I always had—with love, but now, things were different. My instincts told me I had much to worry about.

I started toward the cabinets to grab a skillet for the four-egg, ham-and-cheese omelet he loved so much with just a sprinkle of green onions and red peppers. I kneeled to get the skillet and heard the counter vibrating. When I rose in the direction of the noise, I noticed Howard's cell. He must've left it there when we came in arguing the night before. I picked it up with all intent to just stop the vibration, but my curiosity got the best of me. Just as I pressed the button to see who the text was from, I was startled.

"Baby, I was thinking—" Howard stopped in his tracks as he stood shirtless, glaring at his cell phone in my hand.

His once-delicate face hardened like stone. The fight with him the night before was the longest night of my life. Our morning started off a bit rough, too. And though Howard did everything he could to end things smoothly, it was time to brace myself for round three of a major blowout.

Howard always expressed we would trust each other no matter what. My accusations about the night before, coupled with him catching me spying into his cell phone, would surely light more sparks. I could only hope my marriage would be intact once the fireworks settled.

# Howard

## 4

---

I had to leave there. I jumped in my car and called Kevin to meet me at I-Hop. He kept asking what was going on, but I knew his wife, Melanie, was home, so I didn't want to go into a heavy discussion. This was the first time I ever felt like I wanted to strangle Sydney or do something bad to her, for that matter. The love was still there, but damn, she made me angry. It took some convincing, but Kevin finally agreed to meet me. I made it to the restaurant before he did and waited at our table. He walked in with a smirk on his face and sat across from me.

"Hell, naw, man," I said, shaking my head. "Wipe that grin off your face. If I can't be happy, your ass won't be either!"

"Aw, man, really? That's how it is? And you know you almost got me in trouble this morning, too—calling   me out of the house all early and shit. You know Melanie has plans for me around the house on Saturday mornings. I had to make up some stuff about needing to run a file up to the office real quick, just so she wouldn't be mad."

I slammed my fist on the table. "Man, do you really think I give a f—"

"Hey, hey, Howard . . . watch your mouth. I sense you're about to use Melanie's name in the same sentence, and that's my wife, man."

I bit my bottom lip, took a deep breath then said, "I don't give a fuck," in a low, even tone. "My shit at home is all messed up because of *you* and *your* bullshit, and you want me to care about you being in trouble? You don't even love Melanie!"

Kevin shushed me and glanced around the restaurant, seemingly embarrassed. "Look, man," he said, turning his attention back to me. "Don't say that. I do love Melanie. We're just in an awkward place in our marriage right now."

"Kevin, don't give me that bullshit. Remember I know the whole story. I've been here since you discovered her affair. You haven't looked at that woman the same. You lost respect for her the same day you walked in and discovered her on the phone, crying as she tried to break up with that joker—her coworker at that. So, rest assured I know the truth—you don't want her, but you don't want anyone else to have her either."

"Ex-coworker! I made her quit that mother-fuckin' job. And so, what . . . you judging me now?" Kevin frowned.

"Naw, Kev—"

"Good morning, gentlemen," a young, petite, freckle-faced waitress asked, suspending my rant. "May I get you something to drink?"

"Yes, please," I stated. "I'll have a cup of coffee—extra sugar and cream."

"Sure. How about I bring the items to you, so you can sweeten it exactly to your liking?" She smiled.

"That would be great."

"And you, sir?" she asked Kevin.

"I won't be needing anything," he said. "I have to leave in a minute."

"In that case," I said to the waitress. "I'll just give you my breakfast order now, if you don't mind."

"No problem," she answered. "What will it be?"

The tiny woman quickly scribbled my order on her notepad as if she could tell she interrupted a crucial discussion, and then left in a hurry.

The moments during the interval gave me a chance to calm down before addressing Kevin again.

"Look. All I'm saying is: Are you really doing yourself a favor by staying with a woman you can't love and respect anymore?"

He shook his head. "I can't leave, man." His tone was sullen.

"Why not? You've only been married to her three years, and you don't have kids. Cut her loose, man."

"I know, but . . . you don't understand."

"Understand what? I just told you: You don't want to see Melanie with anyone else."

"No, that's not it, Howard. See . . . Melanie kept telling me I was pushing her away. She begged me to set aside some of my objectives toward my career, so we can work on us and have children. I heard her, but I wanted to keep building my career. And when I didn't get the promotion, she seemed to have lost respect for me. Can you image all the time I spent away from home—only not to get the position I worked so hard for. I left the other company and came to Champion, but the cycle started over. I pushed and pushed again—like I had something to prove. It felt great being recognized for my accomplishments last night, but without Melanie there to support me, I wasn't complete."

His voice was sincere, and I felt bad for him to a    certain extent. "I understand all of that, man," I told him. "It sounds like you feel some responsibility for Melanie cheating, but I'm here to tell you that Melanie knows the rules of marriage just like you do. And any time either of you are at a point where you feel like you need to bang somebody else, you might want to consider getting out of your marriage before somebody gets seriously hurt."

Kevin nodded. "I hear ya. I don't even know what to say to her though."

"You can start by telling her the truth, so I can    straighten my shit out at home."

"The truth?" He frowned.

"Yes, the damned truth! You can start by telling her you've lost respect for her, but you want to gain it back.  Tell her what you did in the restroom last night with Roxie, and—"

"Man, are you crazy?  Who made you the expert on marriages and how to save them?  I'm not telling my wife I cheated with Roxie.  She already thinks Roxie is a whore—"

"She is!"

"Well, that's your wife's friend—"

"Kevin, I will crack yo' cranium with this napkin dispenser if you're saying my wife is a whore."

"Hell naw! I'm saying I wouldn't know Roxie in the first place if Sydney wouldn't have had her around so much. Roxie's had her eye on me for a while now."

"Well, whatever! We're good as long as you aren't saying Sydney is a whore."

"Hell naw, but she's nosey as fuck though. I mean, what made her come looking for Roxie in the first place?"

I shrugged. "Maybe she just wanted to make sure her friend was all right."

"Naw . . . she was being nosey, damnit!"

"So be it. I don't have anything to do with that. Just know that you better tell Melanie something because when I get home, I'm telling Syd the truth. I can't stand being at odds with her, especially when I'm not at fault."

Kevin sighed. "You think Sydney will tell Melanie?"

"You don't have to worry about that. Sydney doesn't like to be the bearer of any kind of bad news. Plus, I'll tell her to stay out of it."

"Cool. Look, I need to run up outta here, but let me ask you something."

"What's up?"

"You kept saying on the phone that you had to leave home before you did something to Sydney. You wouldn't put your hands on her for real, would you?"

I shook my head. "My intentions are to never put my hands on any woman. But after Sydney carried on the way she did when I caught her peeping through my phone, I seriously wanted to choke the hell out of her. It was bad enough to know she didn't trust me, but for her to jump all in my face as if she wanted to kick *my* ass—"

"Whoa, whoa, whoa. Back it up for a second. Sydney was in your face like that?"

"Yeah. I went off—bad—when I saw her with my phone, but you would've thought I called her out of her name, or talked about her deceased momma because she lost all of her cool on me."

"Okay . . . look, man. I'm sorry about all of this. I'm gonna talk to Melanie, and then I'm going to swing by and have a chat with Sydney, too. I'll tell her everything. I didn't mean to jack things up at your house. I'll straighten it all out."

"A'ight. Well, get on out of here before Melanie comes looking for you."

"Here ya go," the waitress said, setting my breakfast and coffee in front of me.

"Damn, that looks good," Kevin said. "On second thought, I don't think I'll be going anywhere." He reached for a slice of my bacon.

I quickly fanned his hand. "Man, you better get your ass on out of here. As hungry as I am, Melanie will be spending her Saturday with you at the emergency room, if you put your paws over my plate again."

Kevin and the waitress laughed. I dug into my food.

"Say your grace, Hungry-ass." He stood. "I'm outta here."

"Peace," I said, my mouth full of food.

# Roxie

## 5

Nigel and I had a long, interesting conversation on the phone the night before. Who would've thought I could have something to talk about with a twenty-six-year-old? I decided I wanted to get to know him a little better. Kevin would just have to understand. Hell, he was married, but I wasn't, so if he still wanted to play, we could. It would just have to be with the understanding that the game had changed. I was going to see Nigel, and Kevin could keep his marriage now that I had something else to tame my interest. Poor Melanie could hold on to her dream of a happy marriage for now—well, somewhat. What she didn't know wouldn't kill her.

I straightened up around the house and lit some candles because Nigel was coming over.

He didn't know it, but I was going to surprise him with dinner. He was only expecting to share some wine and a movie on Netflix, but I had so much more in store for us. He talked a lot of game about how great he was in bed, and a cougar like me wanted to experience it firsthand. Just the thought of his face between my legs set me on fire.

I jumped in the shower after cooking dinner then put on my leopard-print, spaghetti-strapped maxi-dress — with nothing underneath of course. I splashed on a hint of Michael Kors Eau de Parfum in all the areas I knew mattered. Just after putting the top back on the bottle, my doorbell rang. I was surprised, to say the least, because Nigel was early. We agreed on seven o'clock, not six-forty-five. I hurried to the front door then peeped through the hole. I couldn't believe my eyes as I peered at the blur on the other side.

I snatched open the door. "What are you doing here?"

He brushed by me then plopped on the couch. "What's up, baby? I need a place to crash." He plucked off his shoes, using each foot behind the other.

"You what?" I said, standing dumbfounded with the door still open.

He unzipped his pants then relaxed on the couch, propping hands behind his head and his feet onto my coffee table.

"I need to lay low here for a bit, if that's all right with you," he said.

I closed the door then walked over to him. "Um, actually yes . . . Kevin! I do mind! And how did you find out where I live?"

He sat up and stared at me. "Howard told me. What's the problem?"

"Ugh! The problem is I didn't invite you. You've got to leave."

"I can't leave. She found out, baby."

"She who? Found out what?" I was in a panic because Nigel would be ringing that doorbell any minute.

He stood. "Melanie. She knows about us now, and so she kicked me out. Look, I need somewhere to lay my head until things soothe over."

"She kicked you out? Wait a minute. Kevin, we just had sex for the first time last night. How did Melanie find out?"

"I told her."

"You told her? What the—"

"Look, it's complicated. I had to tell her, but give me a little time. Everything will be fine."

I paced my living room. I couldn't think straight. This man literally came to my apartment and made himself welcomed. I was in a bit of a panic because I wasn't sure how to get him to leave just as quickly as he came. I paused in the middle of my living room floor and decided to put it to him plainly.

"Kevin, everything will not be fine because I can't let you stay here. You've got to leave."

He turned—I thought so he could get his shoes, but he followed the aroma from my kitchen. I was fast behind him.

"You cooking, babe?" he asked over his shoulder.

"Kevin, did you hear me? You've got to leave."

He turned to me just after entering the kitchen. "Why? Didn't you hear me say I need a place to crash?"

"Yeah, but why can't you go to Howard's?"

"That man has a wife and family, and you didn't answer me. Why can't I stay here?"

I swallowed hard. "Because I'm expecting company in a few minutes."

Kevin looked taken aback. "Aw, aw, well . . . this is fucked up. Roxie, you told me you weren't seeing     anybody. You didn't have to lie. I'm married. What could I say about you having a man?"

I sighed and stood with my arms folded, trying to decide if I wanted to explain any further. I glanced at the clock on the microwave. Nigel would be outside my door shortly. There was no time for shame, and Kevin still had to go.

"He isn't my man, and I don't usually have company.     I just decided this morning that I wanted to have him over. Now would you please leave, and thank you."

I pulled Kevin by his arm, but he didn't budge.

"So, what . . . you and me last night didn't mean     anything?"

"Of course, it did. It's just that I realize that if you have somebody, I might need to have somebody, too—you know—just to get me through the holidays and such."

He shook his head and walked off toward the living room. "I feel like a fool, you know that? Here I am stuffing bags in my trunk, thinking I could kick it with you for a while, but you done played a playah." He grabbed his keys from the couch.

"Kevin, wait," I called behind him. He turned and looked at me. "I still want you. It just can't be tonight."

My doorbell rang. I dropped my head and sighed. I was hoping Kevin and Nigel wouldn't have to cross paths again, but my hopes were down the drain. Kevin peered at me with sorely disappointed eyes then motioned his hand toward my door.

"Aren't you going to open it?"

I nodded then slowly walked over to the door. I paused briefly once there, crossing my fingers in hopes for a peaceful ending to the night. I opened the door. Nigel stood, smiling, with an armful of groceries and the other hand with flowers. I offered him a piece of a smile then retrieved the flowers as I leaned in to kiss his cheek.

"You look great, beautiful," he said, his eyes sizing me up and down.

I stepped back to let him in. Nigel noticed Kevin immediately. He glanced at me then back at Kevin. I took the grocery bag from him and closed the door. I could only imagine what must've been running across Kevin's mind. And

I'm sure the big bag of Cheetos, Jungle Juice, and gummy bears sticking out of the grocery sack surely didn't help his thoughts much. I didn't know what to do next, so I reintroduced them.

"Um, Nigel, you remember Kevin—from last night, don't you?"

He seemed at a loss for words. "Um, yeah . . . yeah, I remember him." He nodded at Kevin. "W'sup, man? You a'ight?"

"S'up," Kevin responded, half-heartedly. "Yeah, I'm cool."

"Um, Nigel, Kevin was just leaving, weren't you, Kevin."

Kevin's head rotated toward me in what seemed like slow motion. He tilted his head and squinted as he looked at me. His eyes were filled with disbelief. After what seemed like him forever glaring at me, he finally responded.

"Um, yeah. I'm out."

He picked up his gym shoes in one hand and his keys in the other, and then walked toward the door in his socks. I gave Nigel back the items he brought so I could open the door for Kevin.

"Thanks for dropping by, Kev. We'll catch up some other time." I winked at him while my back was to Nigel.

Kevin didn't respond, only walked out the door then turned and looked at me briefly before walking off. I took a deep breath then released it as I slowly closed the door. When I pivoted toward Nigel, he had a look of concern.

"You okay," he asked.

I started toward him and relieved his hands of the snacks. "Oh, yes. I'm fine. What about you?" I headed into the kitchen.

"Yeah. I'm fine." I heard him say.

I pulled the items from the bag and saw that Nigel not only had Jungle Juice and Cheetos, but he also brought a couple of Redbox movies. I dug a little deeper in the sack and was impressed that he remembered from our phone conversation the night before that I like peanut M&Ms and popcorn. I placed the items on the counter then headed back into the living room.

"Well, Nigel, I thank you so much for the snacks, but I hope you're hungry because I made us a hearty dinner."

"Really?" He flashed those pretty white teeth. "I hoped that delicious aroma was coming from your kitchen rather than seeping through your neighbor's walls."

I laughed. "Well, I don't know about where you live, but the walls aren't that thin in my apartments."

"Um-hmm. In that case, I'm excited! That could mean a lot of possibilities for us tonight."

If it was a smile he wanted, he got it. "Is that right?

He winked and pulled me to him. "Shall we eat first?"

"Eat what?" I responded. "Dinner or each other?"

"I like dinner, but I choose the latter."

I giggled and shook my head. "I had to ask, huh?" I took his hand then led him into the kitchen. "Let's just do dinner for now."

As I pulled the steaks from the oven, I felt Nigel watching me.

"What's up," I asked just after setting the steaks on the stove. "Why are you looking at me like that?"

"I was just wondering."

"Wondering what?"

"Is that dude gonna be a problem?"

I took off the oven mitts and set them on the counter. I was a little afraid to answer his question. "You mean Kevin?"

"Yeah. Him. Is he going to be a problem for us?"

I shook my head. "No. Not unless you think he's a problem."

"He's not a problem for me," he answered. I was stunned. "I just thought you might want to know that."

"So, does that mean—"

"I don't care if you're sleeping with him. You're a single woman, and you've already admitted you're not committed to anyone."

"Nigel, I'm speechless."

"I'm not like the average man. Besides, by the end of the night, you won't remember Kevin."

I laughed, but the look on his face was serious. I figured I just better turn around and fix our dinner because there was nothing left to say.

Nigel stood next to me as I fixed us each a plate of T-bone steaks, garlic mashed potatoes, and green beans, slow-cooked with smoked turkey, red peppers and onions, and dinner rolls. I uncorked a bottle of 19 Crimes Cali Red. I learned during our chat on the phone the night before that he was a fan of the Snoop Dogg Blend, so I ran out and bought a bottle for our dinner. I pulled two glasses from the cabinet, and then we went into the living room.

"So, you cool with dinner on the couch, right? I have two folding tables in the coat closet. This way, we can eat as we watch the first movie."

"Sounds good to me."

He complimented my cooking skills damned near between every bite. I wasn't trying to hook the young man with my cooking, but I did want him happy. After all, there was certainly something he could do for me, too.

After dinner, I put up our dishes and the small tables, but we remained on the couch. We finished the entire bottle of wine, shared passionate kisses and were well into the second movie when Nigel slid to the floor and pulled my dress above my waist. He spread my legs wide then buried his tongue deep inside me. He wouldn't come up for air, and I didn't mind. I ran my hands through his silky black curls, gripping a fist full each time he sucked on my pearl tongue. Some young woman had taught him well.

Nigel was right. I forgot all about What's-His-Name and how disappointed he was when he left. Oh, well. After a night like this with Nigel, that other one was going to have to step up his game if he wanted to even look at me again.

# Sydney

## 6

---

I declare makeup sex is the best sex in the world! It was Sunday morning, and I wanted it to last all day. I couldn't remember the last time I climaxed so hard, and Howard wouldn't even let me quit. He bucked into me wildly as my body hunched over, motionless on top of him, gasping for air. I just couldn't move—that is, except for the convulsions he kept sending my body into as I had orgasm after orgasm, shaking uncontrollably. His upward thrusts were relentless, constant, and downright hammered my insides. I didn't think he would ever quit, but it was the warmth of my oozing, creamy nectar that finally sent him over the edge.

"Oh, I feel you, baby! It's so warm!" he said as he quickened his thrusts.

"Ssshh! You'll wake the baby," I panted.

"It's so wet," he whispered. "Damn, you feel so goooo —"

"Ssshh!"

And there he went into a shaking fit. I mustered enough strength to sit up straight on him and grind. I wanted to help him finish.

"Okay, baby, stop," he whispered. "Stop, stop, stop."

"Are you sure," I said, teasing with a slow-wind.

He gripped my waist. "Stop it, Sydney. Shit!"

"Naw . . . I don't think you mean it."

His body jerked, damned near tossing me off of him. "Damn! I'm sorry, baby." He tried to catch his breath. "I'm so sorry."

I rolled off of him. "That's okay. I knew what would happen if I kept going." I smiled.

"You think we woke up, Hailey?" he asked.

"I don't know, but I'll go check."

I rolled out of bed then grabbed my robe from the chair next to the bed. I glanced at my husband, breathless and spent as he lay in the middle of the bed. It felt good knowing I turned him on *and* out that way. As I tied a knot in my robe, I stared at him, thinking how stupid I'd been to think he'd fool around on me, especially with Roxie. My man was a good man. I learned a lesson out of that drama—trust my husband.

The doorbell rang. Howard's eyes popped open, and then he turned to look at me. I shrugged.

"You're not expecting company?" he asked.

"Heck no!" I starting out of the bedroom. "It's too early on a Sunday morning for company."

"You're right about that."

"And it better be important," I mumbled on the way out.

The doorbell rang again as I started down the stairs.

"And get rid of them, quick—before they wake up Hailey!"

*If she's not already awake after all of the noise and yelling you're doing,* I thought to myself.

I nearly ran out of my slippers when I heard the bell chime a third time. Howard was going to be pissed if whoever was at the door woke up our daughter. Sunday mornings was our time to unwind and sleep in. When our pastor introduced a one o'clock worship service after the membership grew significantly, Howard fell in love with attending the later service.

I looked through the peephole and shook my head.

"I don't believe this," I said as I opened the door. "Do you know what time it is?"

"Yeah, it's seven, right?" Roxie said.

"In the morning, Roxie!"

She brushed past me with all her fabulousness and made a beeline for my kitchen. "Well, aren't you up, making breakfast or something?"

"No. Who's up at seven on a Sunday morning when that's the time they have to get up every other day during the week?"

"Well, excuse me then. I didn't know your little routine changed. You used to go running on Sunday mornings and would be back by now."

"Um, that stopped nearly a year and a half ago, Roxie. My daughter is two. I lost most of the baby weight now. I don't get up this early anymore."

"Oh, well, I'm here now. You might as well perk up the coffee pot."

She spun toward the island and set her quilted, tan Saint Laurent shoulder bag on my granite countertop.

I couldn't believe the nerve of her. What she wanted so early in the morning, I didn't know, but I certainly needed to find out. I was right behind her.

"Nice cabinets, Syd. I guess I really haven't been over in a while, huh? And I see you've painted, too. I really like this," she said, scanning the kitchen.

"Yeah, thanks. This was all remodeled back in May—part of my Mother's Day surprise. I came home after having a Sunday brunch with my sister and saw trucks in the driveway. I knew from there what he had to be up to. I only hinted about having the kitchen redone about twenty times." I giggled.

"Wow. And this is American maple, right?"

I nodded. "Just like my mom's old kitchen."

"Wow. Howard is a good man, Syd."

"I know." I went over to start the coffee maker. "What's on your mind, Roxie? What made you stop by?"

"Oh, I figured we need to talk. You know— about Kev and me."

I turned to look at her. She swiveled around on the stool to face me. She stared, apparently awaiting my response.

"You know this puts me in a bad spot, right?"

"Yeah, I know Melanie is your girl and all— your li'l bud, I should say . . . well, things between Kev and me just kinda happened."

"Really? You just kinda ended up in the ladies' restroom together?"

"About that—it was our first and only time, Syd."

"Really?" I said skeptically. I continued prepping the coffeemaker.

"I know you don't believe me, but really it was."

I turned to her again. "So, what is this you think you and Kevin are doing? How far do you think this will go between the two of you?"

"Uuuummm, an honest guess—not far."

"Then, what's the point, Roxie? I mean, why even fool with him?"

She shrugged. "I guess because I don't have a man, and I know he would be willing to give me what I want and what I need, at least for now."

"Look, Roxie. I know you've been hurt by your ex. When we first met, you were very transparent about the pain your ex-husband caused you. But that doesn't give you the right to play around with someone else's man."

"You think I want to marry him? I don't want him to leave her. I just want to borrow him from time to time."

"Oh, like Johnathan *borrowed* Calvin?" I said it before I knew it.

"Now that was low, Syd. You didn't have to go there."

She was right, and I was sorry. "I didn't mean for    that to come out, Rox. Please accept my apology.  I just want you to put yourself in Melanie's shoes. You know what it feels like to be cheated on.  Don't do this."

"You act like I did this all by myself.  Kevin played a huge roll in this, and neither of us wants to fall in love. We're just looking to fill a void."

"Are you serious right now?  He's married, Roxie! Do you know how you sound? Seriously, you are too old for the games you wanna play."

"So, what, darling, I'm forty and fabulous. You better know it."

"But do *you* know it?"

"Yes, I do."

"Really?  I don't think so, and if you did, you wouldn't be whoring like you are."

Roxie jumped in her seat a little.  "Whoring? Well, you just know how to keep the surprises coming.  Tell me, where did *that* come from?"

"I know about the kid from the Madison Hotel, Rox."

"Oh, I get it.  Kevin went crying to Howard, and   Howard told you my business, right?"

I didn't say a word. I pulled two coffee cups from the cabinet then filled them both. Roxie must've been seething as she thought about what I said because once I turned and started toward the island, she ripped into me.

"You listen here, Mrs. Sydney Bland. Not everyone is as fortunate to live your life!"

"My life—"

"Yes, *your* life! You have the perfect husband who loves you, the perfect family life, the perfect career, and perfect home—"

"Roxie, nobody's life is perfect—"

"Well, yours is damned near perfect—you might as well say. You're always looking down on any and everything I do. You think I wanted to leave my man?"

"I didn't say that—"

"I had to! That bastard was cheating—with men at that! I spent years with him, trying to keep him happy, not realizing there was nothing I could do to make him happy. Those precious years of mine were wasted, and I should've been focused on me and my needs. And from now on, that's what I'm gonna do."

"But at other people's expense, Roxie?"

She smirked. "And? I could care less who it hurts or who it half-kills. I deserve my own happiness now."

Just then Howard turned the corner, wearing his    pajama bottoms and a wife-beater shirt. He headed over to the island glancing to and fro at Roxie and me.

"Everything okay down here? I heard yelling," he said.

"Hey, babe. We're good," I said.

"What's up, Roxie?" he spoke.

She gave him an upward nod then stirred her coffee as she poured in some sugar. I sighed, thinking of how sour our conversation became. I turned to Howard.

"Babe, did you check on Hailey? Is she still sleeping?"

"Like a grizzly bear in hibernation." He laughed.

"You're so silly." I placed a soft kiss on his lips. "Babe, will you give me and Roxie a few more minutes, please? I'll be up in a bit."

"What's taking you so long?" he whispered. "I'm ready for round five."

Howard pulled my shoulder, turning me so that my back was to Roxie, and then tugged on my robe.

I giggled. "Babe, stop," I said softly.

"You know I want this," he whispered in my ear. He placed soft kisses on my neck.

"Hold on, babe," I whispered.

He tugged on my robe some more.

"Then, hurry up. Get rid of her," he said in a slight growl, but low enough for just me to hear.

"Okaaaayyy," I said, pushing him away.

Howard started out of the kitchen. "See ya later, Roxie," he said over his shoulder.

"No, you won't," she replied.

Howard stopped momentarily to look at her. Roxie sipped her coffee and never looked back at him.

"Oh, um, babe, would you like some coffee?" I interjected, hoping to cut the awkward silence.

He shook his head. "Nope. I don't need that. But you be sure to have some. The caffeine'll do you some good."

"Get on outta here!" I giggled.

When I turned to Roxie, she wasn't amused. She sipped her coffee again then set it down and grabbed her purse.

"You don't get up this early anymore, huh?" she said.

"Well, you know what I—"

"Yeah, I know what you meant—only when it comes to your husband."

"Roxie, stop being a bitch."

She stared at me through eyes I'm not sure I'd seen before.

"I've got your bitch, Syd." She placed her purse on her shoulder.

"Roxie, wait."

"No, I'm outta here," she said on her way out. "I can tell I've interrupted something anyway." She walked and talked fast over her shoulder. "Pardon the early visitation. I promise it won't happen again."

She opened the door then turned to me.

"Roxie, I wish you didn't feel this way."

"What way? Huh? How am I feeling, Syd?"

I had an answer, but something told me that regardless of what I might say, she would tear my head off. I figured it best to keep silent.

"That's what I thought," she said. "You have no idea what I'm feeling. Go back upstairs and continue riding your man. I'm gonna find Melanie's husband and fuck him. Bye!"

I stood in the doorway and watched as Roxie backed out of my driveway and sped off. Clearly, she was hurting, but I wasn't the reason for her pain. At least, I didn't think I was.

# Howard

## 7

Kevin and I decided to patronize Buffalo Wild Wings N' Things in Southaven, Mississippi since he'd just finished test driving a truck from Landers Ford just up the street. He was undecided about getting the F-150, but he had a minute to contemplate it while they ran his credit and worked on the deal he wanted. I was hungry, so I suggested we get a bite to eat and then head back to the dealer afterward.

"So, you think I oughta get the truck, man?"

I shrugged. "Have you talked to Melanie about it?"

"Look, Melanie barely let me back into the house, and we just don't have much of anything to say to each other."

"Okay, but how do you think it'll make her feel when you come home with a new ride?

That's a major decision to make without first having a conversation with your wife."

He sipped his beer then said, "Well, I guess if I come home with it, that'll give her something to say to me, won't it?"

"Man, I ain't fooling with you." I shook my head. "You couldn't be married to Sydney and get away with the shit you do."

"Well, Sydney hasn't cheated on you either, has she?"

"Naw. She better not."

"I bet if she does, your attitude will change, too."

I shook my head. "Listen. I'm not even trying to think on anything like that. You hear me?"

Kevin's phone rang. He pulled it from his pants pocket then glanced at it. He shook his head just before silencing the phone.

"I'm starting to get real tired of this shit," Kevin said as he set the phone on the table.

"Damn, man, you won't even answer Melanie's calls?"

"I would if she was actually calling me. Hell, that's Roxie's tenacious ass calling me. She's been blowing me up since this morning—like I don't live with my wife. I mean, one minute she's up in

Baby Boy's shit, and the next, she screaming at me."

I chuckled. "Baby Boy? You're talking about the young dude from the banquet? I thought you said she just wanted to make you jealous with him."

"I believe she did. She couldn't possibly want Little Man. I know she wants me, but Melanie let me back up in the house, so I can't be hanging out right now."

"Well, maybe Roxie doesn't know you're back home."

"Like hell she doesn't. I texted her ass last night and told her I went back. You know she doesn't care, right?"

"She doesn't care because she's got 'em lined up and waiting on her. You ain't her only play thang." I teased.

"Well then she needs to quit blowin' up my phone and act like she's got 'em clawin' at her."

"Calm down, Kevin. Breathe . . . breathe, man." I laughed.

I picked up my beer to have a sip, but was damned near choked when I heard the shrill of Kevin's name come from behind us. We both turned and stared at the raging woman, heading toward our table.

"Kevin, who the hell do you think I am?" Roxie fussed.

Kevin's face was priceless—wide-eyes, twisted lips, and a once-brown skin-tone fully flushed.

"Kevin!" she yelled again.

"Um, I think she's talking to you, man. My name is Howard," I stated loud enough for all the patrons to hear. I needed to take some of the shame off me.

"What?" he snapped just as she stopped in front of our table.

"Why aren't you answering my calls?" Her tone was stern and demanding.

"I don't have to answer you—"

"Excuse me, ma'am . . . sir," a tall, clean-cut white man interrupted heading in our direction, "but I'm gonna need you two to hold it down, or I'll have to ask you to leave."

Roxie posed with her hand on her hip. I feared the man had a tongue-lashing on the way, but her tone didn't match her posture. She was rather polite.

"Are you the manager here, sir?"

He stopped just short of our table and replied, "Yes, ma'am. What can I do for you?"

"Well, let me apologize to you, sir. You have a fine establishment here, and I didn't mean to disturb anyone."

"That's fine, ma'am. Just promise me you'll hold your noise to a minimum, so I won't have to ask you to leave."

"Oh, you won't hear another peep," she said. "Just do me a favor and excuse my husband and me for just a minute."

Roxie reached down and jerked Kevin's collar then pulled him from his seat. Once again, he was stunned and held on to her tightly closed fist as he struggled to breathe.

"We need to borrow your lavatory. I promise: This won't take long."

The manager didn't say anything as Roxie lead Kevin into the men's restroom by his collar. Once they were in the restroom, I could only imagine what would happen next. The manager turned to look at me.

I shrugged. "I'm sure they won't be long."

He shook his head then walked off. Just as I picked up one of my traditional wings, drenched in Jammin' Jalapeno sauce, my cell phone rang. It was my wife. I set down the wing and wiped my hands before answering.

"What's up, Syd?"

"Howard, you didn't tell me you were going to Southaven today."

"What?" I paused, surprised by her question. "What do you mean? I told you Kevin was looking for a new truck, remember? And how do you know where I am?"

"Yeah, I remember. I just didn't realize it would be in Mississippi. I'm down here, too. I have some shoes on hold at Dillard's in the Towne Center. I saw both yours and Kevin's cars parked side-by-side in Buffalo Wild Wing's parking lot. I'll swing by on my way out of Dillard's."

I immediately thought about Roxie and Kevin in that bathroom. Sydney would have a fit if she actually saw them together. Apparently, she hadn't seen Roxie's car outside, so I knew I had to deflect her.

"Well, babe, you don't need to do that. I'm not sure Kevin and I will still be here once you leave the store."

"Really? So, you've been there a while already?"

"Yeah, we really need to head back to the dealership to see what numbers they came up with."

"Oh, ok. Well, I guess Hailey and I will just see you later on at the house then."

"Cool. You want me to bring some wings home?"

"No, babe, I'll pass. I'm not sure what I want for     dinner, but we can talk about that later."

"Ok, sweetie. Kiss Hailey for me, and be careful. See you this evening."

"Alright. Love you."

"Love you, too."

*Whew,* was the first thing that came to mind, and then I thought, *Kevin needs to bring his ass out of that restroom so we can get the hell out of here.* There was no doubt in my mind Sydney would drive pass the restaurant on her way back from Dillard's. And what if she spotted Roxie's car then? She would definitely come inside. All I could do was hope and pray the cheaters would be out soon.

I finished off my entire order of wings and fries in a hurry, and then I tried to sit patiently and wait. I started to call Kevin's cell, but noticed it next to his basket of wings and fries as they sat, turning cold.

Five more minutes passed. Ten minutes. Fifteen fucking minutes, and still, no Kevin and Roxie. How does a horny motherfucka not know that when you're fucking off in a public restroom, it should be a quickie? I couldn't take it anymore, so I decided I needed to go bang on the door. Sure, the manager would be pissed, but he would have to just ban me from the restaurant. This was important. The last thing I needed was to be at odds with my wife again, especially over some more bullshit Kevin did.

I stood, heading toward the restrooms. Her sweet voice stopped me cold, sending chills over my body.

"Howard," Sydney sang. I turned to her, slowly. "You said you were leaving. I thought you'd be gone by now."

"Hey, Daddy!" Hailey released Sydney's hand to bear hug my leg.

"Hey, baby girl." I picked her up. "What a nice      surprise, seeing you here."

Hailey giggled. "We surprised you, Daddy."

"Yes, you sure did, baby girl." I kissed her cheek.

Sydney, face still puzzled, set her purse on the end of the table and glanced down at Kevin's uneaten food. My heart sank.

"Where's Kevin?" she asked.

I wondered if she'd seen Roxie's car outside. All I could do was stare at my wife as a million thoughts raced through my brain. Many were of the types of lies I could tell, but most were of how to spew the truth on her.

"Howard," she called, jolting me out of my deep thoughts.

"Yeah, babe?"

"Kevin. Where is he?"

Before I could answer, Kevin stepped out of the        restroom.

"There he is, babe."

Kevin had an aw-shit-type of look on his face, and of course, my wife didn't miss it. She stared him down as he walked over to the table.

"What's up, Syd? I didn't know you were coming. When did you get here?"

"Just a second ago. I was in the area. I saw you two were parked outside, so I thought I'd drop in and say hello."

"Hey, Uncle Kevin," Hailey said, reaching for Kevin.

He pulled her from my arms and she wrapped her arms around his neck.

"Hey, sweetheart. It's good to see you," he said.

Then, Roxie came from the direction of the restroom, smiling as if she'd won a million dollars. I dropped my head and slid back into the booth.

"Sydney, what's up, girl? I didn't know you would be here?"

Sydney ogled her up and down before responding. "Likewise."

Kevin cut the ice. "Howard, I think I'm ready to pack my food to go. I believe the dealership will be calling soon."

"Yeah, I agree. We should head on back over to the lot."

Kevin beckoned the manager over and asked if he could have a to-go container. Sydney reached for Hailey and bid us a good day.

"I'll see *you* at home, Howard."

"See you later, baby."

I tried to kiss her lips, but she turned her cheek. I landed a peck on the side of her face since that was all I could get. I tapped my cheek for my baby girl to plant one on me. She chuckled as she did.

Syd, turned to walk out, and in walked more drama—Nigel. I couldn't believe how this day was turning out. Syd stopped in her tracks, looking more puzzled than she had before.

Roxie belted at Sydney. "Oh, hell naw! I know you didn't just set me up?"

Sydney frowned. "What?"

Nigel walked over to Roxie. "No, don't blame your girl. I followed you here. I guess you didn't think I watch your Facebook page. It's not smart to post lewd pics of yourself with a man sucking your neck in a bathroom stall, and then tag the location, too."

Nigel held his phone out, showing the picture Roxie posted to Facebook. I looked over at Sydney as Nigel swung the image in her direction. Sydney covered Hailey's eyes then hurried out of the restaurant. Kevin was pissed. Just as Nigel swung the image back in his direction, Kevin quickly slapped the phone to the ground. Nigel lunged at him. I stepped between the two men, but it was tough keeping them apart, so the manager jumped in to assist. He held Kevin as I held Nigel back.

"Get off me, man!" Nigel yelled.

"Calm down, bro'," I said, looking around at the terrified patrons. "There are kids in here."

Roxie stood, carrying on as if she was stunned. "Nigel, what in the world is wrong with you? You said this wouldn't be a problem."

"That was before I knew you could take dick back-to-back like I didn't just put it on you. I thought you would at least take a little time off before seeing him again."

"Who are you to tell me how much dick I can have?"

At that moment, Kevin broke from the manager then stood nose-to-nose with Roxie.

"I'm through *fuckin'* with you, Roxie," he shouted. "And I mean that!"

Kevin headed out of the restaurant, swinging the door open as hard as he could. I released Nigel so I could catch up before he could peel off the lot, but I didn't make it. Kevin burned rubber hard. Not only could I hear his tires, but I smelled them. All I could do was hope, he'd be ok.

# Roxie

## 8

I'll admit it was my fault for posting on Facebook, but Nigel had no right to come into the restaurant looking for me. A single woman can do whatever she wants to do. And yes, that's what I got for messing with jailbait. He totally messed up my life. I liked Kevin, but he just stopped having anything to do with me after that day. Sydney stopped taking my calls, too. She might have wanted the friendship to be over, but it certainly wasn't over by my watch. I knew exactly what I had to do to get her back.

I let a couple of weeks go by before I tried reaching out to Sydney again. Of course, she still didn't answer my phone call, so as soon as I hung up, I knew I had to call Howard.

I sat in my car, watching what seemed like a river of water, flowing out of my apartment and down the walkway. I dialed Howard, and surprisingly he answered on the first ring.

"Hello," he said.

"Howard, I know you don't recognize my number, but this is Roxie."

There was a brief pause, and then I heard, "Roxie, how you get my number?" He seemed to have been walking into another room as I heard his background noise fade.

"What do you mean? I'm your wife's best friend. How do you think I got your number?"

"Sydney didn't give you my number. I know that for damned sure so you can try something else. As a matter of fact, I'm about to hang up."

"Listen. Howard," I said quickly. "Just listen, please. I'm in a bind, and I need you guys."

"What do you mean?"

"I messed up. I trusted that dude, Nigel, and he date raped me."

"What the fuck?"

"Yes, and he tied me up while he turned on the        water in the tub and in all of the sinks. He flooded my apartment." I began to fake a cry. "I lost just about everything."

"Roxie, how did you get away? Did you call the        police?"

"A neighbor eventually heard me yelling," I lied. "And yes, I made a police report. I can't even get inside my apartment right now to get anything. The police are still combing the damage."

There wasn't a cop in sight as I hadn't called for one. Nigel hadn't been to my place. He was just an easy cover for the lies I wanted my friends to believe. As for the apartment, by the time this would be over, the apartment managers could just bill my insurance.

"Does Sydney know?" he asked, seemingly concerned.

"She's not taking my calls." I had to put it on extra thick. I cried so hard, even *I* felt sorry for me. "I've been trying to call her. Why won't she answer me?"

"Let me see if I can talk to her. I can't make any    promises but hold tight, Roxie."

"Thanks, Howard."

When he hung up, I looked at myself in the rearview mirror and smiled. I had no regret for flooding the    apartment. I had to flood it in order to keep my lies straight. The apartment complex had insurance, and so did I, but Sydney didn't have to know that. Before long, my cell phone rang. Just as I suspected, it was Syd. I readied myself for a stellar performance.

"Sydney," I cried.

"Roxie, what happened? What is Howard talking about? You got raped?"

"It happened so fast, Syd. He was on me, and I couldn't fight him, and then he tied me up, and he ran the faucets in the tub, in the sinks, and—I mean, I just, I didn't—"

"Wait, wait, slow down, Rox, slow down. Are you hurt?"

"No, I'm not hurt. I mean, at least I don't have any broken bones or bruises, if that's what you're asking."

"When did this happen?"

"It happened earlier this afternoon. The apartment is    a mess. There is so much water damage, Syd. What am I going to do?"

"Ok, listen. Are you sure you're okay? Do you think you need to see a doctor?"

"No, I'm ok. I'm just glad the water didn't ruin my neighbors' belongings."

"Oh, good. So glad to hear that? So where are you staying, Rox?"

"I don't know. I just know even if everything wasn't flooded, I still can't stay here. I don't know if Nigel will come back."

"Well, have you called your insurance? Aren't they going to pay for a hotel or something?"

"No, Syd. I didn't get renter's insurance," I lied. "I never counted on anything like this happening to me."

"So, what are you going to do?"

"I don't know. I don't even know if my job has any type of funds or a program that would help me until I can get another place."

"Oh, Roxie, I really do hate to hear that. My heart goes out to you."

"Thanks, and Syd, I'm really sorry about Kevin. I should have respected you and your friendship with his wife."

"Roxie, I don't want to talk about that right now. I'm just glad to hear you're okay."

"Hey, Syd, you think you can loan me a little money to stay in the extended stay?"

"How much do those places cost?"

"I have no idea. I know those places aren't ideal for me, but it's about the best I can do on borrowed money."

"Did you call anybody back home in Chicago to see if they would help you?"

"Yeah, I did. Everybody's crying broke, you know. I don't blame them though. It's hard to tell what's going to happen with this pandemic and all."

"Roxie, how long do you think it'll be before you can get another place."

"I don't know—a few weeks, maybe. I'm thinking I can borrow from my 401k; you know, a hardship loan."

"How about if I ask Howard if you could stay here for that amount of time? Surely a few weeks won't be a bother to any of us."

If only she could see the grin on my face. It was a good thing our conversation was over the phone because I couldn't help being excited.

"Would you, Syd?"

"Sure. Just give me a moment to talk to Howard, and I'll give you a call back."

I had her right where I wanted her—eating out of the palm of my hands. I don't know why I didn't think of this sooner. If I had, I'd be farther along in my plan.

I stepped out of my car and headed into my apartment. The neighbor on the right side of me got out of his car at the same time and walked up, complaining.

"Hey, what's all this?" he fussed.

"Don't worry. It's under control."

"Are you sure? I don't want my place flooded. Should I call the office?"

I looked at him sternly. "I said it's under control."

He shrugged then shook his head before entering his apartment. I opened my front door then headed inside, squishing water under my rain boots.

As I looked around, I realized I did more than enough damage so that if Sydney or Howard had to come to access things, they could see the carpet was truly soaked. I turned off all of the faucets then prepared to call the apartment emergency line. I need to make them aware that I'd "accidentally" left the water running in my tub all day. Since I needed new furniture anyway, this is what I call helping myself to a blessing.

Before I could dial the emergency number, my cell rang. The caller ID displayed SYDNEY. So, I answered quickly.

"Hey, Syd."

"Roxie, he said it's cool. Get as much as you can, girl, and come on over."

*Come on over,* I thought. My sentiments exactly. It was time for me to go home.

# Sydney

## 9

I knew I should get up, but I really didn't want to. That's what happens when your husband buys you a $5,300 king-sized mattress from the Tempur-Pedic Luxe® collection. Staying in bed all day seems like the best option. Once the pandemic hit, nearly the whole world shut down, so our annual vacation was out of the question for us. And since we couldn't travel, we both agreed to do some things around the house that had been on our to-do list for a while. First thing was to get a new mattress, and boy was I in love with my bed all over again.

I could barely tell it was morning with the blackout curtains still pulled together, but a tiny sliver of sunlight managed to dance through a crack. I stretched and yawned before turning over to stretch my hand across the bed toward Howard. I stretched farther because he didn't seem to be as close to me as I'd thought. But when I still didn't feel him, I opened my eyes and realized he wasn't there.

I sat up in bed and looked at the alarm clock on Howard's side of the bed. 8:00 AM. It was extremely unlike Howard to be up so early. I wondered where he might've gone.

Everything was quiet, but the aroma of Applewood smoked bacon welcomed me into a good morning. *He's making breakfast,* I thought. *What's gotten into him?* I rolled out of bed and slid on my robe before heading to Hailey's room.

I eased her door open, careful not to wake her. I stood in the doorway and just watched her for a minute. My baby girl looked so precious as she slept. I could still remember the moment she was placed on my chest in the delivery room. She was an even mixture of Howard and me in the looks department. Although he tried to say she favored him more, I wholeheartedly disagreed once she opened her eyes and gave me a wide-eyed glare. She definitely had my eyes.

I turned to close Hailey's door, but her little voice gave me pause.

"Mommy," she said.

"Hi, honey, you're awake? I thought you were sleeping."

"I keep waking up and going back to sleep." Her little voice was groggy.

"Oh? Are you ok?"

"Yes." She yawned and stretched. I walked over and kneeled beside her bed to kiss her forehead. "Daddy's cooking breakfast," she said softly, her eyes still closed.

I couldn't tell if she was fully awake or just talking half asleep.

"I know, sweetheart. I can smell it, too. It's pretty early for Daddy to be up cooking, huh?"

"Mm-hmm. Who's that lady he's talking to?"

My heart fell. Hailey reminded me that I brought Roxie into our home the night before. I nearly stumbled over my feet as I stood and backed toward the door.

"Try to get some sleep, sweetheart. It's not quite time to get up yet."

"Where're you going?"

"I'm going downstairs to check on Daddy. I'll be back in a minute, okay?"

"Okay."

I ran downstairs, robe barely fastened, barefoot and all. Once I made it to the kitchen. I noticed Howard at the island, eating a hearty breakfast while Roxie stood in front of my stove dressed in a short, white robe that stopped not only at mid-thigh, but it was sheer enough to see that she had on a pair of hot pink, laced thongs and matching laced bra.

Howard spotted me first. "Good morning, babe."

Roxie turned to face me, pulling her robe tighter. "Good morning, Syd. I'm making breakfast." She pointed at the skillet of eggs on the stove.

"What the fuck are you two doing?"

"Babe, I'm just eating breakfast. What do you mean?"

"Since when did you start waking up to eat breakfast this early?"

Roxie didn't let him answer. "Um, Syd, I'm sorry, but that was probably my fault. Howard only came downstairs because he smelled something cooking."

"Yeah, babe, I was just checking on things, and Roxie asked if I wanted some of the food she had warming already."

"Roxie, you listen to me. Nobody, and I mean nobody cooks for my husband except me! You have no right standing in my goddamned kitchen half-naked, cooking for my husband."

"Half naked?" Roxie said, looking down at herself, "Syd, I'm covered in a robe."

"Bitch, I can see all up and through your bony ass, with your hot-pink lace on. Get the fuck out of my kitchen and find somewhere else to live!"

"Syd, come on," Roxie said, turning off the burners. "I'm sorry. I'm so sorry. I didn't know this robe was that sheer. I'm going to my room right now to find something else to put on."

She placed her hand on my shoulder, and I jerked from her. I wasn't buying it. She couldn't have possibly been that green. Surely, she knew to put on more clothes before stepping out of her room. She wanted to say more, but after I jerked from her, I believe she got the hint. She headed to her room instead.

"Babe, wait." Howard seemed a little nervous, and rightfully so. "I don't want you to get any wrong ideas."

"What other ideas are there for me to get, Howard?"

"Look, nothing was going on, Syd. I know you don't think I would do anything to hurt you, do you?"

"Tell me you didn't notice her ass standing here in her drawers. Tell me that, Howard, and

I'll know you really think of me as a damned fool."

He dropped his head. "Ok. I'm not gonna lie. Yes, I noticed what she had on—or didn't have on. But baby, I promise you, it was nothing to me."

"You can't promise me that, Howard. I don't want to hear that. You're the one who convinced me to call her in the first place. Don't let me find out you and her set up this living arrangement."

"Say what?" His pitch was high. He put his fork down and walked over to me. "Baby, listen." He grabbed my hands.

I jerked away from him. "No, baby, listen, my ass."

Roxie pranced right back into the kitchen with a pair of skinny jeans and a fitted T-shirt.

"I'm so sorry, Syd," she said, hurrying back to the stove. "I know I keep saying that, but really I am. I had no idea I put on the wrong robe. I was just trying to cover up."

She quickly stacked some eggs, bacon, and pancakes on a plate then set it on the island close to me.

"I made you breakfast, too," she said. "Bon appetite!"

"Are you serious right now?" I said, walking toward her.

Howard grabbed my arm. Roxie stood shaking her head as if she didn't know what was going on.

"Syd, what's gotten into you? I said I'm sorry."

Howard had me by my waist now. "I heard what you said, but did you hear me? I said get the fuck out of my house. Did you hear me that time? Huh? Can you hear me now, bitch? Can you hear me now?"

"Ok, Syd," Howard said, turning me to him. "Look, nothing happened. Roxie admitted she was out of line, and she apologized."

"Yeah, Syd. I swear I didn't mean to upset you, and I didn't mean to disrespect you either. You've been good to me. You're the last person I want to hurt. Please believe me. I'll never even step foot in the kitchen to cook again. Just please give me another chance."

I stared at her, unblinkingly—trying to stare a hole into her soul. I wanted to believe her, but the truth was I really didn't. She and my own husband were making me out to be the villain, and there was nothing I could do about it. That pissed me off.

I glanced at the beautiful breakfast she set on the island in front of me. And before I knew it, I splattered it onto the floor with one swoop of the hand, shattering the plate and all. I jerked from Howard and turned to leave the kitchen and was stopped cold by the sight of Hailey in the entrance, trembling with tear-stained cheeks.

# Howard

## 10

I sat in my office, staring at the 5x7 picture of Syd and I on the beach in Montego Bay, Jamaica. It was one of my favorite photos of us, so I ordered a silver Michael Aram Calla Lily frame and set it on my desk the moment I returned to work. We chose to vacation in Jamaica for our fifth wedding anniversary and stayed ten days. We could do that because it was before Hailey was even thought of. After our baby girl was born, our getaways included her.

As I stared at the picture, it dawned on me. *Maybe Sydney took on a friendship with Roxie as a way of having something in her life that didn't include Hailey and me.* Maybe we were smothering her. I really didn't know.

There were no ifs, ands, or buts about it— Roxie had to go! A little more than a week went by after the breakfast incident, and my wife's mind was gone. She appeared to be in deep thought daily. Each morning she barely let me kiss her before leaving for work, and at night, she moved my hand when I wanted to go under her nightgown. When I asked if she wanted to talk about what was bothering her, she declined.

This behavior had to be about Roxie. I only agreed to let her stay with us because Syd insisted in the first place. My gut said it was a foul decision, given everything I knew about Roxie, but I was put on the spot. Syd asked me out of the blue and made it seem like I had to give her an answer right away—like it was a matter of life and death. For all I knew, Roxie's situation really was dire.

It just seemed odd that the Nigel guy was bold enough to cause thousands of dollars in damages to property that didn't belong to him and risk going to jail. But that was exactly where he was going. Roxie was sexy and all—something I'd never admit to Sydney—but regardless of how fine any woman is, jail just ain't worth it!

I never could understand why Sydney valued her friendship with Roxie so much. From the very start, when Roxie began working in the same bank, I tried to warn Sydney about befriending her.

"I'm telling you, Syd. She doesn't come off as a woman who can't make friends," I said just after opening the passenger door for her.

I picked up Syd this day because her car was in the shop. I took a personal day off to handle some banking business, so there was no need for her to rent a car. Once my business was done, it was time for Syd to get off work. When she saw me standing in the door of her office, she picked up her desk phone and dialed someone, stating to meet us outside so she could introduce me.

I opened the door for my wife to exit the bank and felt someone very close on my heels. I turned around once outside, and before I could say anything, Roxie grabbed my hand and kissed it. I snatched away, and the women laughed. I walked on to the car, and Sydney caught up.

"Howard, you're hard on everybody. It seems like every time I meet new people you have a problem with them. Tell the truth: you don't want me to have any friends, do you?"

I gasped. "Woman, get in the car. Just get in the car."

Syd giggled then slid into our BMW. I walked around to the driver side to get in. As I opened the door, I looked up and noticed Roxie standing in the door of the bank, eyeing me. The brief exchange of eye contact was eerie as her eyes seemed to be stating something sinister. I quickly hopped into the car.

Sydney went in on me. "You should just admit it. I make friends easily, and you don't."

"That's non-sense. Syd, all I'm saying is, you can't bring everybody home with you. There are different classes of friends."

I checked my mirrors then pulled out of the parking space.

"What? Howard, I've never heard of that."

"Listen. Some friends you meet at church, and that's where you socialize with them—at church. Some friends you make at school, and that's the extent of the friendship—at school. Some friends you meet at work, and—"

"Let me guess, and that's where you leave them—at work."

"Exactly!"

"So, who do I bring home with me?"

"Syd, you have to take your time and get to know people. Give it some time, and you'll learn that not everyone you thought would be a friend are truly friends."

"But you haven't given Roxie a chance. I'm telling you: she's hell-a cool. She's intelligent and funny, I mean look how she just kissed your hand. You should've seen the look on your face. That was funny as hell! She's so cool and —"

"And that's enough about her. I don't want to talk about her anymore," I said. I could see Sydney's puzzled face in my peripheral as I drove. "Now what I want to talk about is my wife. How was your day, baby?"

Although my last statement softened Syd's face and sort of lightened the mood, I could tell she still had questions. I said what I meant, but Sydney was determined to have Roxie around, so I just had to go along with it. Roxie was the new girlfriend Sydney would be shopping with, going to happy hour, and gossiping on the phone late at night.

Kevin barged into my office, abruptly snapping me out of my daze. "What it do, man?" He closed the door behind him then took a seat in front of my desk.

"I called you over an hour ago. I thought you'd never come. Geez!"

"Why? What's wrong? No, wait. Let me guess: You screwed up the Walworth account again?"

"Heck no. I'm good on that. In fact, this isn't even work related."

"It's not?" Kevin leaned in.

"No. This is a bigger fish to fry."

"Word?"

"Yeah, and her name is Roxie."

Kevin slid back in his seat. "Man, what's this got to do with me?"

"She's still at my house, and I need her gone."

"Again, what's this got to do with me? Melanie and I are good, and I intend to keep it that way."

"Remember what I told you about her when she first came into the picture?"

Kevin raised an eyebrow and slid back in his seat. "Yeah?"

"Listen. This ain't a good look, man. I need her up out of my house."

Kevin stood and started backing toward the door with his hands up. He shook his head. I had to stop him.

"What? Where're you going?"

"Howard, I ain't fuckin' with that chick. You see what she did the last time I was with her? The woman got issues. She's crazy, loco, coo-koo."

"I know that. You know that. Hell, I believe the whole world knows that. But Sydney for whatever reason didn't understand that until Roxie started living with us."

Kevin couldn't seem to stop shaking his head. "It's been what—a week?"

I sighed. "Yeah."

"Yo'! You got a lot of nerves." Kevin threw up the Black power fist. "Be strong. I can't do nothin' fa ya, bruh. I'm sorry, man."

Kevin turned and opened the door. I yelled for him to come back, but he was gone quicker than I could say, "Hey!"

I plopped down in my seat, feeling defeated. I missed my wife's smile and her bubbliness. There had to be something I could do to cheer her up until we could get Roxie out of the house. All I could do was try one more time to see if she would open up to me about how she was feeling. In the meanwhile, I needed to pull an old trick to soothe her over until I got home. I picked up the phone and dialed my assistant.

"Ms. Karen, I need a favor, please. Will you find a flower company with same-day delivery? I need two dozens of mixed roses sent to my wife's job."

"I'm on it, Mr. Bland."

# Roxie

## 11

It was a beautiful day out, so I called in at work. I told my manager I forgot I needed to be in traffic court that   morning. She excused me for the day, considering I told her I had no idea how long I would have to be there. I was a long way from Downtown Memphis, where my so-called court appearance was supposed to be. I headed to another familiar place. Somewhere people knew me, and still liked me.

First Area State Bank was the workplace I once called home after submitting multiple resumes and finally being chosen for an interview. The job was good to me for the eighteen months I worked there. I left because I got what I came there for.

As I pulled up to First Area State Bank, I noticed a florist delivery van in the parking lot. As the man opened the double doors in the back, he pulled forward a bouquet of the most beautiful roses I'd ever seen. Breath-taking would be an understatement. They were nearly fully bloomed, and the assortment of colors were so vibrant, all I could do was gravitate toward them.

I quickly got out of my car and walked over to the    delivery van catching the man off guard as he turned around.

"Oh, crap," he said as he jumped. "You startled me, Ma'am."

"Well, my momma used to have an old saying when that happens. She would say you must not be living right, if someone could startle you that easily."

"Huh?" the wrinkly, blue-eyed gentleman said.

"You know. When you're doing wrong, and someone walks up on you, it scares you."

He still didn't seem to catch my drift.

"Never mind," I responded.

"May I help you?" He still seemed puzzled.

"Yes, I was just wondering if you are about to deliver those roses inside the bank?"

The man looked around. This time, I noticed the slight hump in his back as the years hadn't been kind to him. He turned back to me and squinted.

"Well, yes, this is the only facility on the lot. I don't reckon it's another building behind this one, is there?"

I refused to let his sarcasm get the best of me. "You know what. I see your truck is full, so why don't you let me do you a favor and take those in for you."

"Who are you?" He looked me up and down.

I wasn't wearing a badge, but I gave it a shot anyway.

"I work here, and the bank isn't currently letting anyone inside without an appointment. You know—due to Covid-19."

"Oh, you work here."

"Yes, I'm the manager as a matter of fact. Which one of my staff members are the roses for? Wait. Don't tell me. Are they for Sydney Bland?"

He glanced at his clipboard, and then at the box the vase sat in and replied, "Yes, ma'am, they sure are."

"I knew it! Her husband does things like this all the time."

"Okay, then if you'll sign right here, I could be on my way."

I used his pen to sign the board, scribbling a fake John Hancock. I returned the pen, and he handed me the roses. *Oh, I'm good—too good*, I thought. How lucky was I to have pulled up about the same time as the delivery driver? I couldn't have planned it better if I had tried. The bank was nearly empty when I walked in, but every teller and desk had someone in front being served. My former co-workers smiled and waved at me as I strutted by with the large vase. I said hello to the branch manager as I passed her office on my way to Sydney's office. She called out to me, so I turned back.

"Hey, Tina," I said, leaning in her door. "How are you?"

"Hey, Roxie. I'm good. What do we have here?" She stood and stepped around her desk.

"Oh, these are for Sydney."

"Wow, how nice!"

"Yeah, I thought so, too. It's good seeing you. Let me get these in there to her, so I can get out of you all's way."

"Okay," she replied, walking toward me.

As I walked away, I glanced over my shoulder and saw her standing in her doorway, watching me. Sydney's office was only a few doors down. I knocked and lifted the roses so that they covered my face.

"Come in." She sounded as if she was asking more so than making a statement.

The moment I stepped in, I lowered the roses and discovered a what-the-fuck look on her face. How she got her eyebrows to nearly meet while bucking her eyes, I'll never understand. I immediately attempted to put her at ease.

"Sydney, look. I'm only here to make peace. Things have been odd between us lately, and it really shouldn't be. We live together now, and we don't even speak. I'm really hurt by this."

I set the roses on her desk and noticed a small card stuck inside them. I quickly snatched it out before she could see it and placed it into my purse.

"Roxie, you really didn't need to—"

I interrupted her. "Syd, no one is more deserving of these roses than you."

"Thank you. They are very beautiful."

"I thought so, too." There was an awkward moment of silence between us before I said, "Sydney, listen. What do I need to do to make things right between us again?"

"I don't know, Roxie. I've been asking myself that, and I'm really not sure."

"And that really hurts me because I truly miss my sister from another mister."

That got a slight giggle out of Sydney.

I kept tugging on her heart strings. "I sort of thought us living together would be fun. You know late-night chats over tea, chick flicks, even us cooking together, sharing recipes."

"All of that would have been great, but at this point—"

"Really, Syd? It's been eight days. There has been no interaction between us since the first night I moved in."

"Roxie, you tell me how you'd feel if you walked in on your best friend, barely dressed, laughing and joking it up with your husband."

"Syd, you think I haven't thought about that. I wish I could take it all back now. I realize how it looked. But, girl, you know Howard loves you. I wasn't trying to seduce your man either. But even if I was, he doesn't want anybody but you."

"That's not the point, Rox."

"I know. I know. I do get it. The point is I was out of line. I don't know how many ways to ask your forgiveness. But I wish you would forgive me. I love you, girl. And that's why I'm moving out."

Until that moment, Sydney's eyes were fixed on something outside the window. She heard "moving out" and threw her neck and head around to look at me so fast, I figured she had whiplash.  The excitement in her tone disappointed me.

"Really? You found somewhere already?"

"Yeah, but calm down. It won't be ready for another month."

Sydney's smile quickly faded.

"Hey," I said then took a seat in a chair in front of her desk. "I totally understand your frustration. "You want your house back—just you, your hubby, and your baby. But you know apartment managers usually wait until the applicant has been approved before preparing the place   for the next tenant. And you should feel some kind of comfort that I'm leaving."

"Well, yeah."

"Although, I know it's not soon enough for you."

We both giggled.

"And check this out." I held out my hand for her to see the sparkling beauty on my ring finger.

"Roxie, what's this?"

"A wedding set."

"Yeah, but what does it mean?"

"Relax. It's not real. I just thought it was cute. I saw it at Walmart, and I also figured it would keep men from trying to push up on me so quickly. After my issues with my ex-husband and

Nigel and Kevin, I'm just done dating for a while. It's time for me to enjoy my singleness. I'm looking forward to moving into my new place and moving on with my life."

"Roxie, that's the best thing you could have ever said. I'm really proud of you."

"Thanks, Syd. By the way, there is one more thing you can be proud of me for."

"What's that?"

"I'm being awarded the Five Star Recognition at my company's banquet this evening. It would mean a lot to me if you and Howard would come."

"Tonight?"

"I know it's short notice, but we haven't been on speaking terms, and I just couldn't fathom the two of you not being there to celebrate with me."

I could see her wheels spinning in her head. I was hopeful she was trying to figure out a way to say yes.

"Well, you've always been there for us, so let me see if my sister, Teresa, will keep Hailey tonight."

I leaped with excitement. "Thank you! Oh, I really hope your sister isn't busy."

"Me, too. After all, you were there for Howard's recognition. I'll give him a shout to let him know we have a hot date tonight."

I'm glad it didn't take much convincing. Sydney seemed to have let her guard down, which was totally my plan. I listened on as she called Howard to talk about their so-called hot date. Little did she know, the hot date would be all mine.

# Howard

## 12

I don't know if I'll ever understand women. My wife, after having been distant and of very few words for more than a week, called to inform me we would be going to an awards banquet to celebrate Roxie's accomplishments at her job. What the hell got into her was beyond me. She didn't even sound like herself. I didn't think the roses I sent her could have changed her mood so drastically. Oh, and speaking of roses, she never thanked me for sending them. She used to enjoy receiving flowers on the job. I dismissed the fact that she didn't acknowledge my act of kindness because I was glad to hear her upbeat for a change. We agreed I would take Hailey to Teresa's house, which I did, and then I headed home to shower and shave.

I pulled out the same black tux I'd worn to my awards banquet. I placed the garments on the bed and the shoes on the floor at the foot of the bed. Sydney walked into the room, smiling.

"Hey, you," she said as she set her purse on the bed.

"Hey, you, yourself."

She met me for a kiss.

"So, you're going for black? I think I want to wear a red dress."

"Sounds good to me." I stared at her for a minute as she headed into the closet. "Babe, it's good to see you feeling better."

She walked out of the closet, holding up a sexy, red spaghetti-strapped dress.

"I am," she sang.

"Mind if I ask what happened?"

"I sort of feel like I'm getting my life back. Roxie found a place."

"Wow. That was quick. I'm happy to hear that."

"Only catch is, it won't be ready for another month."

"Aw, damn, but at least she has a plan to get out of here, right?"

"Right." Syd held the dress by the hanger, high into the air. "What do you think?"

"It's beautiful. I can't wait to see you in it."

"Me, too. I went shopping a few days ago, trying to get my mind off things. I didn't know I would be wearing it this soon."

"It's very sexy, babe. In fact, it's making me feel some kind of way right now."

I brushed against her backside, letting her feel how stiff I quickly became. I kissed the back of her neck and nestled my hand between her thighs.

"When will Roxie get here?" I asked, spinning her around to face me.

"I don't know. Who cares?" She kissed me hard.

"Let's take this to the shower." I led the way.

We spent at least half an hour in the shower, making up for lost time. I wasn't sure if there would even be hot water by the time Roxie could get in and take a shower, but I didn't care. I missed my wife, and she certainly proved how much she missed me as she traced my body from head to toe with her soft, warm tongue. Sydney knew how much I loved it when she kneeled, taking me whole into her mouth while the water ran on top of her back, her shoulders, and her head. So damn sexy! She never let up until I was barely standing, winded, and filling the acoustics in the bathroom with animalistic groans.

Though very weak and damned near needing oxygen due to the heavy steam caused by both my panting and the hot water, I was more than happy to return the favor and pleasure my baby. She let out the sweetest moan at the first touch of my tongue. Her moans fueled me to give her more, so I took a deep breath as I gripped her ass and pulled her into my face. As I buried my tongue deep into her vaginal walls, her legs trembled and soon they fell weak. I tried to hold her up as she began to slide down the glass wall.

Sydney's moans were intoxicating. I didn't want to stop, but I knew if I didn't, we would be lying on the shower floor, too weak to get up and possibly drowning from the force of the shower head. Syd was spent, and I knew it. I opened my eyes and was startled by what appeared to be a figure in the distance, staring at us through the fogged shower glass. I quickly got up.

"What the fu—" I said, standing to wipe the glass clear.

Syd quickly turned to look as well. "What? What's wrong?"

If someone was there, they had disappeared by the time I cleared the steam on the glass. "Oh, nothing. I thought I saw someone. It must've been your dress   hanging on the door. I didn't realize you hung it there."

"Oh, yeah. Sorry."

I kissed her lips. "You good?"

She smiled then kissed my lips. "Oh, I'm better than good."

"Really now?"

"Yes, really."

"Ok, then I guess if you wash my back, I'll wash yours."

"You got it," she said.

I turned and let my wife pamper me with more kisses and a nice massage with the soap suds. I couldn't help but think about what I thought I saw. I didn't want to alarm, Syd, but I was pretty certain the figure had to be Roxie. Things were starting to get eerie, but I could only hope for the next few weeks or so to go by quickly. My wife was right. We needed our life back.

Syd and I got dressed then headed downstairs to meet Roxie. As Syd passed by her bedroom, she placed her ear to the door.

"She's in the shower. I hear the water running," she said.

I laughed. "Well, that won't be a long shower. I'm sure we used all of the hot water."

Sydney and I joked about our shower playtime as I held her hand to help her down the stairs. We went into the kitchen and discovered a tray of strawberries, three champagne flutes, and a chilled bottle of Veuve Clicquot, sitting in a bucket of ice. Sydney picked up a note written on a yellow-lined journal page.

I listened as she read it aloud. "Wait for me. I'll be down shortly. We're riding together in style as I have arranged for a limousine pickup."

"A limo?" I said in disbelief. "You've got to be kidding me, right?"

"No, that's what the note said. We're going in style."

I couldn't believe what I heard, but hey, it wasn't my night. It was Roxie's affair, and if she wanted to arrive in a limo like it was prom night, who was I to judge it. I cracked open the champagne and poured some for Syd and me. We toasted to us and to having a beautiful life together then began to drink.

"I wonder if they'll have a red carpet, too," I said, jokingly just after taking another sip from my glass.

"Oh, wow. Babe, you know that would be right up Roxie's alley."

Sydney and I shared a laugh.

"Ah, you two know me so well," Roxie said, startling us as she entered the kitchen. "I couldn't convince the office to throw in a red carpet, but you know I tried, right?" She laughed.

"So, you got them to pay for the limousine?" Syd asked.

"No, that was all me and my big idea. I think I deserve it. You know many events are still cancelled due to Covid-19, so there aren't many places I can go to dress up like this and have a car service."

"True," I said.

Roxie picked up her glass and fussed. "And can't the you two read? My note said wait for me. I wanted to toast with you."

Syd's glass was half empty and so was mine. Roxie took Syd's glass right out of her hand and offered to pour more.

"Here. Let me get you some more. And go over there next to your husband so we can all toast."

Syd walked from the other side of the island over to me. I admired her in the little sensual number she called her new dress. This was the first time I'd seen her in something so erotic, but I didn't mind at all.

"Roxie, doesn't my baby look stunning?" I kissed her lips as she walked over and slid her arm around my waist.

"She absolutely does. I was just about to ask where ever did you find that dress? It looks like something I'd wear."

Syd and I shared glances before she responded. "Well, I'm not sure what to say behind that. But if you're offering a compliment, thank you."

"Oh, indeed," Roxie said, handing Syd her refilled glass of champagne.

She reached for mine next. "Don't fill it up."

She paused to look at me before pouring. I didn't understand the drooping expression on her face. I couldn't tell if she was surprised that I didn't want more to drink or if her feelings were hurt. After all, she partied her butt off when I was being recognized for my accomplishments at work. I knew she wouldn't let it go and just do what I asked.

"And why not? You're not driving. I made sure of that, so we would all have a good time."

I felt a little bad. Sydney and I had been more concerned with each other than about the whole reason we were dressed up in our kitchen having champagne in the first place.

"Well, Roxie, that was nice of you," I said. "Really, all of this is a nice touch. I don't mean to seem insensitive on your big night. You deserve this recognition as Sydney   has always said you had a lot to bring to the table at both companies."

"Aaaawww, thanks, Syd. You never told me that. It's such a beautiful thing to have friends. You all have been so good to me. I know I'll miss you once I leave, but at least we all love each other, right?"

Syd and I looked at each other. Like me, I believe she didn't want to respond. Neither of us answered, but instead, I offered an interruption for the awkward silence.

"Hey! So, are you just gonna  hold my glass, or are you gonna pour me some more champagne?"

Roxie smiled. "You got it, mister!"

Sydney bit into a strawberry and took another sip of her champagne. My body temperature seemed to rise with each one of her bites — not to mention how my mouth watered. I sucked on my bottom lip as I watched my wife in all of her sexiness. When I turned and noticed Roxie staring at me, I quickly shook my thoughts of devouring Syd and opted for a strawberry instead. Roxie nodded and smiled, seemingly pleased that we obliged her treats. The strawberries were very good though, and so was the champagne.

Roxie wouldn't stop talking. I understood her excitement as I recently had been in her shoes. To receive any type of honor is great, and when it's done in a profession you love, it feels amazing.

As Roxie continued talking to us, her voice faded in my head as I zoned in on Sydney. She was seated at the island, and she didn't look well.

"Babe, are you okay?"

"I don't know," she said, rubbing her stomach. "I think I might've eaten too many strawberries."

Roxie came closer. "Syd, you okay? You don't look well. You're perspiring."

She was right. Sydney's hair was pulled off her face and into a bun as it was all she could do to get ready quickly after having wet it in the shower. Tiny beads of sweat pierce her forehead and nose. I'd never seen her like this, so I was in panic mode.

"Sweetie, listen. Anything hurting you? Are you   having any pain?"

She shook her head. "No. I just think I might need to go to the bathroom."

Roxie picked up a piece of mail off the kitchen counter and began to fan her. "Oh, so you really think it was the strawberries? Are you allergic?"

"No. Well, I don't know. At least I don't think I am," Syd answered.

Just then, Roxie's phone rang. She answered her cell, and I turned my attention back to my wife.

"Baby, let's get you upstairs. We don't have to go out tonight."

"It's the limousine driver, you guys. He's here," Roxie said. "What should I tell him?"

"Hold on, Roxie," I pleaded as Syd stood. We headed out of the kitchen toward the stairs. She held her stomach. "Baby, you gonna make it? Do I need to carry you upstairs?"

"No, baby, I got it." Her voice was faint. She whispered in my ear. "I just think I have to have a BM."

"Are you sure, Syd," I whispered back. "A bowel movement now? If that's all, then maybe the driver will wait."

"No, sweetie." Syd looked at me as lovingly as she could and said, "I can tell this is going to be a while."

As Syd rounded the corner into the hall, I was close behind her. I asked Roxie to pardon us for a moment. She nodded, still holding her cell to her ear. Syd stopped just at the foot of the stairs and took a deep breath before parting her lips to say something. I didn't give her a chance to speak first.

"Baby, I'm not going without you," I demanded in a tone that let her know I meant what I said.

"You have to, Howard. Look at all she's gone through for this, and she didn't invite anyone else. Who will she have to support her tonight?"

"The rest of her coworkers," I said, matter-of-factly.

"Howard—"

"Hell, I don't know. It doesn't feel right going without you, Syd."

"I know, baby. Listen, once I'm done, I'll drive myself. You all go ahead. I'll ride with Roxie on the way back, and you bring the car home."

I wasn't ok leaving my wife behind, but at the same time, I knew she was right. Roxie had no one else to support her, so I had to stand in the gap. I should have known I would regret it.

# Roxie

## 13

It worked! My plan actually worked, and I had the darling, Mr. Howard F. Bland III, all to myself for the night. I never thought I'd admit it, but growing up in a dysfunctional household had its advantages. I grew up around a family full of heartless, liars, manipulators, thieves, and self-absorbed people. My own mother never even cared about how I felt day to day. I never knew my father, but my mother brought plenty of men in and out of my life who at least pretended to care for me. I knew their affection wasn't real, but just like those men, I pretended that it was real long enough to get what I wanted. I figured faking it worked for my momma, so why couldn't it work for me.

I recall needing bus fare to get to school, so I wouldn't have to walk. I hated walking in the winter or when it rained, so I asked one of my mother's Johns if he would give me bus fare for the week. He pulled out a couple of twenty-dollar bills, and said they were mine—but only if I let him look at it. "It" being my who-ha. Since that was all he wanted, I didn't see anything wrong with letting him see it. I hopped into his Lincoln Continental, and he drove around for nearly a half hour, jerking off as I sat in the front seat, spread eagle with my back to the window. I was sixteen then, and at that point, it was the worse that could've happened to me.

I learned from some of the best in my family how to scheme my way into getting what I want. Then, by some grace of the stars and the heavens above, I went off to college at eighteen. I met a wonderful, God-fearing man named Frankie who became a great friend and by our sophomore year, we were in love. I truly didn't deserve him, and more importantly, he didn't deserve me or my dishonesty. I wanted to be good to him, but I wasn't sure if I even had it in me. I had grown to love scheming and lying.

I kept more money on campus than any-body—all just by sleeping with some of the shy boys at the school. I knew not to deal with the bad boys. That could get me caught. But the quiet ones—the nerds—the ones nobody wanted, I figured as long as they paid me, and I kept them satisfied, my secret would remain safe. I could smell a virgin a mile away. I went after them with no mercy, making sure to get them sprung so I would have them feening for me. Some of them spent all of their book money on me. At times I felt bad, but they would justify it by saying they would borrow a classmate's books.

These guys all knew I was in a relationship, but they also thought they were the only "other" one. A few of them started thinking they were in love with me, so I tried to slack off a bit. I never told anyone how I managed to keep money without work study or a regular job. My boyfriend thought I was braiding hair on campus—at least that was the lie I told him. I managed to keep it going for three years without him knowing. It was our senior year when he finally found out and broke it off with me.

One of my tricks saw me going into a dorm with another man and later addressed the guy to find out if his suspicions were true. They both turned on me, telling Frankie, and no matter what I said, he believed them. Frankie said everything they said added up while my story had holes in it.

It was hard seeing him on campus. He wouldn't even look at me. I was devastated to lose him. I vowed to be a better person from that point on. Only thing though—the old saying of what goes around comes around actually came and bit me. Years later, I fell in love with a terrific man and married him, thinking I had a new lease on life. We were married several years before I discovered his infidelities—with men. I was hurt, but I also had to come to the realization that perhaps I had it coming.

Losing my husband sent me back into the world-wind of a woman I used to be, and now I was back up to my old tricks. I told my coworkers that I'd recently gotten married— hence the fake wedding set I bought at Walmart. I couldn't help myself. Everybody kept talking about the awards banquet and what their husbands were planning for them, VIP seating and such, so I felt left out when someone asked if I would have a date.

"Date," I laughed. "Um, ye-ah. Why would you think I wouldn't have someone on my arm on the night I'm being honored?"

There were four of us in the breakroom, having lunch. Due to social distancing, we each were at our own small table.

"Well, you never talk about anyone, so I assumed you aren't dating or in a relationship." Amanda's freckled-face-ass seemed to love making people feel smaller than her.

Freckles made some people prettier. Not in Amanda's case. Or, maybe it was just that I didn't like her attitude so I conveniently picked apart what I viewed as her flaw. Either way, I didn't like her ass. Yes, she had a husband, so I refused to let her keep getting one up on me, especially with other women in the office sitting there, listening.

"A marriage is more than a relationship, darling. I thought you knew that, being married yourself." I smirked.

"Wait. You're married?"

"Close your mouth, sweetie," I said, sternly. "Not everyone goes around broadcasting their business in the office."

"But, when you first started here a year ago, I thought—"

"See, you shouldn't think so hard. Your thinking was more like assuming."

Amanda just wouldn't let it go. "But you don't have pictures of you and your husband on your desk. You don't even wear a ring, so naturally, anyone would assume—"

"Honey, did anyone ever tell you about assumptions?" I stared at her as I held a pregnant pause. "They make an ass out of *you*, not me."

I politely packed my remaining lunch then stood to leave. I turned to the small audience once again.

"Oh, and just in case any of you are still wondering—my wedding set is in the shop being upgraded for our ten-year anniversary."

I walked out, and five days later, showed up to work sporting what could have easily been taken for a three-carat, halo princess-cut, two-piece wedding set. Price? A whole eighty-three dollars plus tax. It was a white sapphire set on sterling silver, but who would tell anyone any different? Certainly not me.

Back to getting what I wanted. I wanted— no—I *needed* Howard to escort me to the banquet. How else was I going to get him to agree to come with me alone besides poisoning his wife? I didn't want her dead—yet, so I only dropped a few squirts of a fast-acting, liquid laxative into her champagne to keep her at home. I knew it would do the trick, but I also made double-sure Sydney wouldn't make it to the banquet by hiding her car keys. In the short time I'd been living with them, she misplaced her keys three times. Why she didn't have a permanent spot to place them, I don't know. But this day, it cost her because I placed them where I knew she'd never find them — deep behind several large items in the pantry. I went upstairs and heard them in the shower, so I took advantage of that time to let the air out of one of Howard's tires. Once I was done, I went back upstairs. I walked into their room and feasted my eyes on Howard, apparently working a magical tongue between Sydney's legs. I seared with envy. Yet, I was frozen in place. I couldn't take my eyes off of them.

When Howard noticed me, I darted from their room and quickly made it into my own room. Oh, how I wanted him. I needed him. And there was no doubt in my mind, I would have him. I jumped into the shower and masturbated, imaging Howard relishing my goods just as he had with Sydney. The water quickly turned cold, snapping me out of my erotic fantasy.

Howard was awfully quiet on the ride to the banquet. He mostly fidgeted with his cell phone. I knew he was texting Sydney. He seemed worried about her. He sat on the far end of the car, which pissed me off. He even respected his wife when she wasn't around. I had to break the ice.

"Everything okay, Howard?"

"Um, yeah. I think so." He didn't bother to look up.

"You're texting, Syd, right?"

He kept his eyes on his phone. "Yeah. Just making sure she doesn't feel any worse."

"I understand. I really hope she's okay."

I slid closer to him. That got his attention. He looked at me as if to ask what I was doing. I ignored the curiosity on his face and began rambling in hopes to get his mind off Sydney.

"You know, Howard, I'm really glad you're going with me. I mean, I hope Syd makes it, too, but you're both my friends, so I'm just happy that at least one of you were able to come. Oh, and I paid for VIP seating, so we'll have a private table, a special dinner menu, and more champagne. You could use some more champagne, right? I know I could. My nerves are all over the place. I mean, I have no idea what I'm going to say for my acceptance speech. Well, I'll keep it short. It's just that—"

"Um, Roxie . . . Roxie. Breathe."

I paused momentarily, and then we both laughed.

"I'm sorry," I said.

"I knew you're excited. I guess I'm the one with the nerves, considering I left my wife at the house feeling ill."

I brushed his shoulder. "I'm sure she'll be ok."

Howard was busy looking at my hand rubbing his shoulder when his phone lit up with a text from Sydney. It read: YOU THINK SHE LACED MY DRINK? MAYBE SO. I'M STILL ON THE TOILET! When I noticed his eyes move to his phone, I turned my head and looked out of the window.

I could only respond to Sydney in my head. *You goddamned right I laced your drink! Your man is mine tonight, bitch!*

Once we made it to the venue, the driver stepped out and opened our door. Howard got out of the car, and in true gentleman fashion, he reached for my hand and helped me out as well. Just as I had hoped, Amanda and a few other ladies along with their spouses stood only a few feet from the limo. I could only imagine what went on in their heads as they noticed my "husband" and I exit the car.

Amanda and all her messiness couldn't wait to walk over and introduce herself. I latched on to Howard's arm and leaned in to give him a quick word.

"This bitch is nosy as hell. Keep your responses short with her, so she'll go away. Better yet. Just let me do most of the talking."

Amanda stepped to us with the fakest smile I'd ever seen. Her husband was close behind.

"Roxie, you look beautiful as always," she said.

"And you just always look," I quipped.

I don't think she was ready for that. She stood, seemingly not knowing what to say next. Her husband took over from there. He reached to shake Howard's hand.

"Hi. I'm Richard, Amanda's husband."

"I'm Howard, Roxie—"

"Listen, why don't we take this inside?" I interrupted, walking away.

I grabbed Howard's hand and pulled him close behind. I felt him squirm a little in an effort to release his hand, but I held on tightly. I nodded at a couple of other ladies on the way into the building, but I didn't stop to chat. Once inside, Howard managed to jerk his hand from me and in doing so, he noticed the fake wedding set.

"Roxie, what's that on your hand?"

"What do you mean?" I didn't bother to look at my hand.

"That," he said, pointing. "On your ring finger. Is that a wedding set?"

"It is, but it isn't."

He rubbed his hand over his head then glanced around the room. "Roxie, you didn't—" He paused then looked around once more. "These people don't think—" He took a deep breath then returned his attention to me. "Please tell me these people don't think I'm your husband."

I shrugged. "I can't control what somebody thinks."

"Roxie—not cool, man. This shit ain't cool at all."

I stepped closer to him and whispered. "Howard, I only bought this ring after Kevin and I stopped seeing each other. And after what happened with Calvin, I just didn't want to seem available to anyone for a while. I'm not ready to date. But my coworkers don't know about my life outside of work. I've never shared with them whether I'm married."

"But you do realize how this looks, right?" He still didn't seem relieved.

"Well, yeah, I do," I said. "But that'll all be cleared up once Sydney gets here, right?"

"Syd!" he said, digging in his pockets for his phone. "I need to check on her."

His phone was tucked safely inside the backseat of the limousine. The last thing I needed was for him to be distracted on *my* night. He seemed to be a little panicked by the fact that he didn't have his phone.

"Relax, Howard. I'm sure your phone is on the backseat of the car, and it'll be there once the driver returns."

"He left?"

"Yes, but he knows what time to be back here. Chill out."

"But I need to check on, Syd. Give me your phone."

"I don't have it. I accidently left it on the island," I lied—well at least the accident part was a lie. "Look. Let's just go over to our table. My category is supposed to be called first after dinner. We can leave then. I'll use someone's phone to call the limousine company to let him know when we're ready."

Howard sighed heavily, sounding as if it was all he could do to keep from crying. But he soon relented.

"Where's our table," he asked, looking around.

I took advantage of his guards being down to move in and embrace him. I hugged him lovingly, knowing someone from my department had to be looking. He smelled amazing, and his hard, chiseled body felt even better. I inhaled, taking in all of his enchanting aroma. Though he didn't immediately embrace me back, it could have appeared that he was hugging me when he put his hands around my waist briefly to ask me to release him.

"Okay, Roxie. I'm ready to get to our table. You can let go now."

"Gladly."

I brushed my lips across his neck before pulling away then shot him a quick smirk. He was playing hard to get, but the night was still young. There was no doubt in my mind that by the end of the night, my legs would be securely wrapped around his waist in the back of the limo. And what a ride it would be!

# Sydney

## 14

I sat up in bed, staring at the clock as if it was a ghost. 1:03 AM. *Un-fucking-believable!* I thought. *How could Howard still be out with her at this time of morning and not check in with me.* I must've dialed his phone twenty or thirty times. *Where the hell is he?*

I started to think trusting him to go ahead without me was a bad idea. I didn't imagine I would be stuck on the toilet for half the night either. Howard even texted me with concerns that Roxie could've put something in my champagne because there was no real clear reason for the sudden illness.

By the time I felt better, I was sure dinner at the banquet was served, but I still wanted to go. I wanted to get there before the actual ceremony began. I headed downstairs to the kitchen where

I remembered leaving my keys, but I couldn't find them. After about twenty minutes of searching, I decided to take Howard's SUV. I grabbed his extra set of keys from the kitchen drawer, and then attempted to reach him on the phone again.

"You've reached the voicemail of Howard F. Bland III. I'm sorry I'm unavailable right now —"

I was frustrated beyond belief. My blood pressure had to be rising as I was livid. I quickly headed to the garage, got into Howard's truck and started it up. I pressed the remote to lift the door and placed the SUV in reverse. The garage door raised to the top, but before I could back out, the tire light came on. I hopped out and notice a flat tire on the back passenger side. *Damn it!* I thought. *How many things can go wrong in one evening?*

Calling my sister was an option, but I decided not to have Teresa get out with Hailey tagging along. By 8:45, I took off my dress and got into bed. I figured an hour or two more, Howard would be home. Boy was I wrong!

As I lay in our dark bedroom, trying not to fry my brain with woulda, coulda, shouldas, I watched the red numbers projected on the wall from our, LED digital clock repeatedly turn. 1:23

AM. Finally, the sound I'd been waiting for snapped me out of the mental torture. It was the chime of the security alarm as the front door opened and closed. Their faded voices in the distance singed me. Then there was a brief crescendo in their tones just before one of them drew a loud "Ssshhh!" Everything went silent once again. Their soft footsteps tapped the hardwood stairs. I wanted to jump out of bed and lunge at them, sending us all flying down the stairs.

Howard entered our bedroom, barely making noise as he unbuttoned his shirt. He didn't bother to look over at me as I pierced his skull with my eyes. I couldn't take it anymore. I turned on the lamp on my nightstand. Howard jumped.

"Babe, what are you doing up?"

"Oh, did you really think I'd be asleep, Howard?"

I hopped out of bed and started toward him.

"Baby, look. I know this looks bad, but let me tell you what happened."

He reached for my hand, but I snatched from him.

"There ain't shit you can tell me that will make a difference."

Howard tilted his head and squinted. "So, I can't talk? You ain't gon' let me say nothing?"

"It's 1:27 AM. That says it all!"

"Look. Lower your damn voice."

Howard walked over to the partially closed door and peeked out. He seemed to be satisfied that Roxie wasn't in the hallway, so he pulled himself back in and softly fastened the door.

His tone was low. "Syd, believe me—I was ready to come home the moment we arrived to the place."

"Howard, don't give me that. You need to come with some other lie if you want me to even consider what you're saying."

"Ok, so since won't let me explain, then I'm done with it."

"Really?" I was floored.

"Syd, I know you had a rough night, but did it ever occur to you that mine might not have been so great either?

"I've been trying to reach you. Why didn't you call me to let me know how things were going?"

"Somehow, I left my damned phone in the limousine."

That sounded like a well-thought-out lie. "The limo? Howard, you are not that irresponsible."

He shook his head and sighed. "Goodnight."

He started to walk around me, but I placed my hand in his chest, halting him.

"Where do you think you're going?"

"I might as well get ready for bed since you clearly don't want to hear what I have to say. We both have to work in the morning."

I couldn't believe he tried to shut me down. How dare he come home at an ungodly hour, after being out with my best friend, and then think he had the right to close the conversation.

"How would you feel if I came home at this hour and didn't call to let you know what was going on?"

"Syd, I feel like we are going in circles. Let's talk about this in the morning."

"We both work in the morning, Howard."

He sighed heavily this time. His eyes swirled around as if he was fishing for what to say next. I stepped closer to him and grabbed his hand. Her scent assaulted my nostrils. I couldn't help doing a doubletake, and as I did, I noticed lipstick on his neck and collar. He must've known what I was about to do because his reflexes were immaculate.

He caught my hand mid-air as I tried to land a blow that would not only devastate him, but more than likely hurt me, too.

"What the hell—" He squeezed my hand.

I struggled to free myself. "You got that bitch's perfume on you, and her lipstick is on your neck!"

"Her perfume? I don't know what you're talking about, Syd."

"Get out!" I screamed.

"Sydney—"

"Let me go, Howard! Get out!"

"I'm not leaving my house, Syd."

"I don't care. You're not getting in bed with me. Get the fuck out!"

"Here you go with this shit. You think I slept with her?"

"I don't know!"

"I tried to have a conversation with you, Syd, but you didn't want to fucking talk, so forget it."

He let me go and started toward the bathroom.

"Let me take a shower, and I'll be out of your way. I'll go sleep in my baby's room."

I didn't try to stop him. I climbed in our bed and cried until my face hurt. Once he got out of the shower, I heard him go down the hall to

Hailey's room and close the door. I wondered how he would rest in her toddler bed, but even if I wanted to peek into the room and see, I couldn't because I heard the rustling of the knob as he locked the door.

I knew I wouldn't get much sleep afterwards. I lay in bed, thinking about how I would address him in the  daylight hours. I also continued to talk myself out of attacking Roxie on her way down the stairs for work. So much had been done that made me question whether she was the problem or whether it was just me being the overthinker. Either way, I damned near hated her, and I wanted to hate myself more for bringing her into our home. Things couldn't possibly get any worse, at least that's what I thought.

# Sydney

## 15

The morning was tense. Howard woke up, running late for work, so not only did he blow right by me as I got ready for the day, but he didn't bother to pick up our conversation from over in the night. I heard him downstairs, yelling on the phone with AAA to get a technician out as quickly as possible as he was already late for work. I wanted to go tell him that it wasn't AAA's fault he had a flat tire.

In all his yelling, he eventually hollered up the stairs to tell me he found my keys behind some items in the pantry. I couldn't recall going into the pantry, but then figured evidently I did.

"Thanks. Set them on the kitchen island, please," I shouted, giving him the same rude tone, he gave me.

That was all he actually said to me before leaving the house.

I only had a few winks of sleep and really wanted to call in for a personal day, but that would only ruin my perfect attendance at work. I called Hailey to say good morning, made a light breakfast sandwich with turkey sausage and eggs, and then headed to work.

Roxie had long gone. I heard her leaving before either of us got out of bed. That made me feel as if she didn't want to face me, but then I realized though she didn't talk to me face-to-face, she certainly didn't mind calling. I'd only been in my office for about twenty minutes when the desk phone rang. It was her number on the caller ID.

"This is Sydney Bland," I answered. "How may I help you?

"Good morning, Syd."

"How may I help you?" I was cold.

"I know I'm the last person you want to speak to, but I needed to call and let you know that you don't have to be angry with Howard about anything."

"You've got a lot of damned nerve, calling me, Roxie, but since you did, talk."

"Well, I know how it looks, Syd, but you've got to know that Howard was the perfect gentleman."

"Roxie, when I say talk, I mean get to the chase."

"Ok. Let me be straight up.  Howard was ready to leave long before the awards ceremony began.  I had no idea my category had been pushed damn near till the end of the program. To make matters worse, he managed to leave his cell in the limo, and when I checked to give him mine, that's when I realized I had to have left mine at the house as I was in a hurry."

I had to give it to Roxie. She was good at explaining things. Her well-put-together thoughts were almost convincing.  I still challenged her.

"So, you didn't know anybody who would lend you their cell phone?"

"Syd, we were in the middle of the ceremony. Our   table was upfront.  Who would have let me take their phone out of the banquet hall to use it?"

"Hell, I don't know, Roxie, but as your friend, I wouldn't have ever been out with your man that long with no communication."

"I totally understand, but if you don't trust me, surely you trust Howard, right?"

I thought momentarily then answered. "How did he get lipstick and perfume on him, Roxie, and don't you lie to me?"

She sighed heavily and then took a brief pause before responding. "You got me there, Syd."

"What?" My heart skipped a beat. "What did you do, Roxie?"

She sighed again. "I hugged him. When they called my name, I pulled him to me and squeezed him tight. I had no one else I could celebrate with. I noticed that as other nominee's names were called, their responses were to hug and kiss the people they brought with them. I didn't want to look awkward, so I grabbed Howard and latched on to him."

"You kissed him?" I asked almost in an inaudible whisper.

"No, I only hugged him, and when I pulled back, somehow my lips must've brushed his collar."

"There was lipstick on his neck, too, Roxie."

"Syd, I didn't see that. If there was, and I believe you, I'm sorry. I didn't mean for that to happen. I just wanted to feel like I had someone there who was really proud of me."

I can't explain it, but somehow, she did it again. Roxie had successfully made me relax my guards. I told myself I would once again hate myself if I let down my guard, but I still loved

Roxie. She had some difficult ways, but all-in-all, she had been a good friend. It was only recent that our friendship started to look different. My silence piqued her interest.

"Syd?"

"I'm here, Roxie. And for what it's worth, I *am* proud of you."

I could hear the smile in her voice. "You are?"

"Yes. I'm very proud of you."

"Proud enough for drinks after work? I was thinking you could round up the ladies at the bank for happy hour like we used to."

"Yeah. That actually sounds good."

"Good. Then I'll meet you back at the house. We can ride together."

"No, Roxie, let's just meet straight from work. If I go home, I might change my mind."

"Yeah, you're right. So, I'll see you at Bonefish Grill in Cordova?"

"Yeah. That's cool."

"Good then. I'm so excited! This way, I get to celebrate with you after all."

"Right. See you there."

I hung up, wondering what I'd just done.


I pulled up to Bonefish Grill's parking lot around 4:45 PM. Happy Hour was from 4:00 to

6:30, and fortunately, my workday ended at 4:00 PM. As I sat in the parking lot, mixed emotions ran through me. Roxie had always been over-the-top from the day I met her. She was outspoken, confident, and always went after what she wanted. She left First Area State after having only worked there for eighteen months because she saw a better opportunity with another bank. I admired that about her. Me—taking leaps of faith wasn't so easy. Before I'd apply for a job, I needed several conversations in prayer and with my husband in order to feel better about jumping into a new endeavor. Unlike Roxie, I'm also a more behind-the-scenes type of person. I despised being in the spotlight. Yes, I could make friends, but there weren't many I'd bring home with me.

My mixed feelings were about the fact that Roxie had done more than enough to show me that I'd outgrown our friendship. So, did I really need to break bread or have drinks with her? She and I seemed to be in different head spaces. She had become a fun-girl, partying, sleeping with married men, and sleeping with strange younger men, while I enjoyed quiet movie nights with my family. Having her in my home showed another side that let me know her level of respect for me was nonexistent. Yes, she apologized, and yes, I believe people can change. However, she was way too comfortable in my home and around my family than she needed to be. This was just another side of her that needed to be revealed, so I would know how far to go with our friendship. She needed to leave my home—point blank—period.

I decided that since I was in the parking lot, I'd go inside the restaurant and have one drink. Roxie invited some of the ladies from my current office, so I didn't want to disappoint them. As I got out of the car, I spotted one of my associates, Rita, heading inside the restaurant with Roxie. I entered only a moment later. They turned and noticed me.

"Hey, girl," Rita said. "We haven't done this in a while, huh?"

"No, we haven't. Leave it to Roxie to get us out."

Roxie giggled and then turned to ask the hostess for a table.

I glanced around the restaurant, noting the ambiance hadn't changed. It was dimly-lit, cozy with two fireplaces, brick walls, cloth linen on the tables, and candles throughout. The heavenly aromas flowing from the kitchen suddenly made me hungry. I tuned in to the back-and-forth conversation Roxie seemed to be having with the hostess.

"Yes, ma'am, I know, but is your entire party here?" the hostess asked.

"No, but everyone is on their way," Roxie responded. "We just left work."

"I'm sorry, but I won't be able to seat you unless everyone is present," the young brunette responded.

"But we're trying to take advantage of Happy Hour. They might not make it until closer to 6:00."

"I'm sorry, ma'am, but I won't be able to seat you    unless you are all here."

Roxie didn't seem to like her response. She turned to us frowned up like she'd licked a lemon.

"Excuse me a second, ladies. I see a friend over behind the bar."

Roxie sashayed across the room, making it to the bar in what seemed like three steps. She shared brief smiles and giggles with a woman who was picking up drinks for a table. The woman nodded then Roxie returned over to the front of the restaurant.

"We're about to be seated, ladies," she said.

"But Trina and Lisa aren't here yet," Rita said.

"It's ok. My friend is getting the ok from the manager to seat us."

Just as Roxie said, the manager, a tall, dark, and lovely drink of water, stepped to us and ushered us to a large booth.

We were ready to order drinks before even looking at a food menu.

"I need something with vodka or rum in it," Rita said.

"Oh, rum and pineapple juice sound good," I said, looking at the drink menu.

"First round of drinks on me, ladies!" Roxie said. "Now let's get this order in before the rest of the crew shows up."

We laughed. Roxie beckoned the waitress she'd spoken to previously.

"Ladies, this is Ashley, a good friend of mine. Ashley, this is Rita, and this is Sydney." She pointed to each of us during the introductions.

"*Oh*, this is Ashley," I said. "You all went to UT Martin together, right?"

"Yes, that would be me," Ashley said.

"Oh, cool. It's so nice to finally meet you. I've heard nothing but great things about you."

"Okay. I was just about to say it was all lies, but since you heard great things, I'm all in agreement. Whatever Roxie told you—it's true!"

We shared laughter with her for a moment or two. Ashley was a nice-looking woman with a personality very similar to Roxie's, having never met a stranger. She was talkative and had a great sense of humor.

"What will you ladies have?" she asked. "And please know this is my side gig, and a very much-needed-gig at that. In other words, I'm going to serve you right because I need my tips to be on-point."

"Well, all right now," Rita said, "I heard that."

Ashley took our orders and was back very quickly. Before I knew it, I had downed my drink, and the waitress was dropping off another one along with a few plates of appetizers. Another waitress helped serve our table.

"Wait, what's this?" I asked. "I didn't order another drink, and who ordered the appetizer plates?"

"I ordered the appetizers," Roxie said.

"And I ordered another round of drinks for us," Rita said. "I hope that was okay. You aren't ready to leave, are you?"

I was a bit uncomfortable because I truly didn't want to be there much longer. But I didn't want to seem like a party-pooper, so I nodded.

"It's ok. I guess one more drink can't hurt."

Just then, Trina and Lisa walked up.

"You better have another drink," Trina said. "We just got here. What do you mean, you guess one more can't hurt?"

"Hello, ladies," I said as they slid into the booth.

"Where's our waitress," Lisa asked, looking around. "I'm ready to get this party started."

"Have some appetizers," Roxie said. "They're on me."

"Now this is my type of party," Trina teased.

Six-thirty came and went, and we all were several drinks in. I forgot how good it was to have a girls' night. We laughed, played the dozens, sang old songs, offered professional advice, and more. It truly felt like a women's bonding night. I was set and ready to offer the women to do another hang out over the upcoming weekend. But then, we got on the subject of marriage, dating and men. That's when things went far left.

"I'm just saying that if a woman can take a man from another woman, then that man wasn't truly hers to begin with," Trina said, rolling her eyes.

"But if it's a marriage, it's totally different, Trina," I said. "Regardless of what you say, a marriage is a union and a covenant between God, that woman, and that man. If he cheats, that means he broke the covenant, but it does not discount that he was ever her husband."

Lisa took a gulp of her drink then set the glass on the table. "So, what if it's the woman who cheated? You know we cheat, too. I'm just sayin'!"

"I still feel the same—it doesn't change the fact that a covenant was created," I answered.

"Ok," Roxie started. "So, what if the woman wasn't married to him?"

Roxie's friend, Ashley, walked up at that moment with a tray, and began setting another round of drinks on the table. I continued with my answer.

"If they weren't married, and she cheats, I don't know why he would want to keep her nasty ass anyway." I took a sip of my drink.

Ashley spoke up. "Oh, you're just saying that because *she* had *YOUR* man." She pointed at Roxie.

The entire section of the restaurant hushed. If a pin had dropped on the floor, I swear it would have been heard. I could only imagine the horrific look I displayed as it felt like a thousand tiny needles pierced my skin simultaneously. I glanced around the still restaurant. Trina, Rita, Lisa, and even people from other tables nearby seemed to all have gaping mouths. I managed to compose myself and turned to Roxie.

"What the hell is she talking about?" I demanded more so than asked.

Roxie set her glass on the table and dropped her head. "Syd, um . . . listen . . . I, um—"

"Spit it out!" By now my chest heaved, and I trembled with anger. "Is it true?"

"Yes, but it was—" Roxie started.

I jumped up. Roxie flinched. "Let me out!" I screamed. "Let me out of this fuckin' booth!"

Roxie slid out of the booth. All the while, she kept trying to get me to listen.

"Syd, wait. I need to explain."

"Roxie, I don't need to hear shit you got to say." I grabbed my purse. "I knew your ass was shiesty!" I pointed in her face. "I don't know why I ever trusted you! Don't bring your ass back to my house. I'll pack your shit and put it on the doorstep."

I stormed out of there in a fury. My first mind was to call Howard, but I opted to see him face-to-face instead. A phone conversation wasn't going to do for this one.

# Roxie

## 16

That damn Ashley! She totally ruined my plan. I told her to keep her mouth shut. Maybe I should have let her in on my whole scheme, but I didn't know if I could fully trust her. I wanted to get Howard between my legs one more time before letting Sydney in on our secret. I knew once Sydney found out that Howard and I had been together, she would be angry enough to leave him. That most certainly would wound him, and he'd come running to me—the woman he never could get enough of.

Ever since the night of my awards banquet, I had visions of me straddling him, riding him into submission. He didn't know that I actually told the limousine driver not to come back until midnight. Once the ceremony was over, the party continued until 11:00. The banquet hall cleared out, so we went outside to wait for the limo. Howard was restless, checking the time on his Movado every few minutes or so. He was furious that our car still hadn't shown up and insisted on calling an Uber. I kept assuring him that I'd spoken to the driver on a coworker's cell phone, and the driver was on his way.

It was a quarter past midnight when our car pulled up. Howard was so busy giving the chauffer a piece of his mind that he didn't see me motioning to the driver not to respond. I put my finger to my lips and shook my head. Thankfully, he kept a straight face. Howard was so angry, he forgot his manners and jumped into the limousine before me. I took that opportunity to slip the chauffer a couple of Benjamins for his trouble and whispered to him.

"Take the long route home—at least an hour."

I climbed in then sat next to Howard, trying to spark a conversation. He was utterly rude. All he seemed to have on his mind was Sydney. He didn't want to talk to me about anything but that boring-ass wife of his. I tried to bring up some of the funny moments of the night, hoping to get a giggle, a smirk or something. Instead, he closed his eyes and began to dose off.

I waited until I heard him breathe heavily, making sure he was asleep before making a move. I even heard a faint snore. I pulled up my dress, exposing my panty-less bottom and straddled him. He must've been a little tipsy because he didn't move or feel my weight on him until I kissed him. He slowly opened his eyes and stared into mine. I knew I had him. He wrapped his hands around my waistline and squeezed tightly. I gasped and embraced myself for what I knew was going to be one hell of a ride.

Sydney told me back at the restaurant not to come home, but whether she meant it or not, I was going back. I had things there that belonged to me—including Howard. As I pulled up to the house, I saw Sydney's sister driving away. She didn't see me because she was busy looking in the rearview mirror as she apparently spoke to Hailey in the backseat. I figured she tried to drop Hailey off and was sent away, which could only mean one thing—Howard and Sydney were fighting.

Her sister must've been in a rush to get Hailey out of the house because she left the front door slightly ajar. I could hear loud arguing as I approached the porch. I stepped just inside the foyer and listened on as Howard and Sydney yelled at each other in the kitchen. I didn't close the door because the chime of the security system would alert them of my presence.

One thing I could say about Sydney was that she was a loyal friend to everyone she'd befriended—including me. In all fairness, I didn't make my move on Howard sooner because of her. The poor thing really believed I was her friend. She clearly was devastated to finally confirm that I was not.

"I don't know what to fucking believe anymore," she cried. "My husband and my best friend—the two people besides my daughter who mean so much to me—lied to me! You lied to me, Howard!"

"How did I lie, Sydney? I didn't lie about anything."

"You fucked her, and neither of you were upfront until this shit blew up on you!"

"You act like that was recent or something. Sydney, it was such a long time ago."

"It doesn't matter how long ago it was, Howard. You were supposed to tell me from day one. Instead, you made a pact with her not to tell me."

"Syd, you were gun-ho about this new friend at work. The day you introduced us, for some reason, I couldn't get it out. I was just shocked to see that my old girlfriend from college was the woman you had taken a liking to. How was I supposed to tell you?"

"Like you did just now, damn-it! All that time I talked about her, you didn't think one time to tell me you dated a woman named Roxie in college?"

"The woman I dated was named Roxanne! We never called her Roxie."

"And that bitch is good! She needs an Oscar. She never once fucked up and called you Frankie. If she had, I would've known something because the only people who call you by your middle name are your friends from high school and college."

"Syd, you've got to believe me. If she had ulterior motives from the start, I didn't know. Hell, she slept with my best friend. Why would I think she came back here, all the way from Chicago, to do something foul?"

"I just thought of something. What if she only came back here to befriend me, trying to get close to you? Think about it. The woman you described to me from college was conniving."

"It's been more than fifteen years since I last saw her, Syd. If that's true, her ass is crazier than

I thought. When we graduated, she spent a few more years in Memphis, and I'd see her at events, but we didn't have anything to do with each other."

"Did you ever get tested for anything after you broke up with her, considering you said she was turning tricks for money?"

"Of course, I got tested. I told you I met another girl, and I knew I needed to make sure I was safe for her."

"You told me about your other college girl-friend. Why didn't you ever mention Roxie?"

"Because I hated her. I erased her ass! As far as I was concerned, she didn't exist. She played me—upset me so bad, I knew I'd never hurt a woman like that. I tried to forget every memory of Roxanne. That's why I felt like I saw a ghost when you introduced me at the bank. Last I remember, she moved back to Chicago."

"Well, she ain't no ghost, and she's not welcomed back into our home, Howard."

"That's fine with me. You're the one who wanted her here in the first place, remember?"

"Yeah, but I wish you would have put your foot down about not letting her in. She's torn my house apart. We've never argued so much. I'm putting her shit on the curb tonight!"

I couldn't take any more. I rounded the corner and entered the kitchen.

"I don't think so. You didn't bring my shit in from the curb, and you're *not* going to sit them out there."

Howard was the first to speak. "Why did you come here in the first place, Roxanne?"

"Hmph. So, now I'm Roxanne?"

"Roxie, Roxanne, or whatever the fuck you want to be called—why are you here?"

"Well, *Frankie*," I said, moving closer, "you both were right. I came back here for you. I wanted to have a happy life, but I married the wrong man. You were supposed to be my husband, and I still believe I deserve that chance."

"Have you lost your goddamned mind?"

"No, Frankie, but I realize how much I must've hurt you because you lost *your* mind when you let me go. People in their right minds know how to forgive and move on. You should've given me another chance."

"I didn't owe you shit then, and I don't owe you shit now! Get the fuck out of my house."

He stepped around me as if he wanted to go toward the front door. I slid into his way.

Sydney was on the phone by then, calling the police.

"Or what, Frankie?" I stepped even closer. "Hmph? Are you going to sling me across the room like you did when you picked me up by my waist and tossed me in the back of the limousine?"

"You're lucky that's all I did to you for straddling me and putting your fucking lips on me."

"You used to want these lips. You used to tell me I was the most beautiful woman in the world. I kept my body and appearance up for you. I knew someday we'd be back together. After my divorce, I realized my time was now. I'm a better woman than the girl I was in college. I was good to my ex-husband. Frankie, we need a do-over."

"Woman, even if I weren't married, I wouldn't have you. Just in the little time you've been in Sydney's life, I've seen the real Roxanne — the same one that had me believing I was the only man for her. You've got a serious problem."

Sydney's voice distracted me momentarily as she came off strong and adamant as she spoke to the 911 dispatcher.

"Please tell the police to hurry because I know I'm about to catch a case. If she puts her hands on my husband, she'll wish she hadn't when I get through with her!"

It seemed like only moments had passed when I heard sirens creeping closer to the home. I was furious with Sydney.

"So, you gon' do me like this, Syd? I thought we were friends."

"Bitch, you only pretended to be my friend, and I'm over you. Now you need to get out of my house."

"This is my house, too!"

Loud banging on the opened front door startled all of us. I glanced around the corner and noticed a policeman knocking with his baton.

"Police!" he announced.

"In here, officer," Howard called.

Four police officers charged into the kitchen.

"What's going on," the tall, husky brunette asked.

Sydney gave them her version of things and told them she wanted me out of her house.

"Once again—this is my house, too!" I claimed.

"She's right," another officer replied as he lifted his cap and adjusted it over his neatly groomed fade. "Once you allow someone to move in, you can't just throw them out."

"How do I get her out of my house?" Sydney seemed panicked.

"You'll have to take her to court to have her evicted."

"But she's causing problems. I'm afraid one of us is going to end up in jail." Sydney slammed her fist on the island granite top.

"Look. We can recommend her to leave, but we can't make her unless she's been violent—in which then we can take her to jail. Has she touched either of you?"

"No," Sydney and Howard said in unison.

"Then, there isn't much we can do." The brunette turned to me. "Ma'am, for the sake of keeping the peace, will you consider leaving tonight?"

"If I leave, they might change the locks, and I won't be able to get the rest of my things. She even threatened to put my stuff on the curb. What happens then? Will you arrest her?"

"No, she won't be arrested, but you can take her to court, if she does."

"Then I'm not leaving."

Sydney had a fit. She paced the kitchen as she loud-talked the police. Howard paced with her, trying to calm her down. He stopped her by wrapping his arms around her, whispering into her ear. She collapsed into his arms. I was beyond green with envy. I loathed her. I wanted to be her in that moment, wrapped in Frankie's arms.

"I'm just saying!" she cried. "I let her into my home, feeling sorry for her after she was attacked, and this is the thanks I get?"

"Attacked? When were you attacked, ma'am?" the brunette asked, turning toward me.

My stomach sank. "Oh, it was a while ago."

Howard turned and responded. "It wasn't that long ago—a few weeks, maybe."

"Who attacked you, ma'am," another officer asked.

Sydney felt the need to answer for me. "This young guy she met at a banquet hall where my husband was being honored on his job. She invited him into her home, and he raped her, tied her up and destroyed her apartment. She reported it the same night. It happened in the New Farmington Rock Apartments."

The brunette asked, "What's your full name, ma'am."

"Roxanne Mills," I responded meekly.

One of the officers pulled his mic off his shirt then walked toward the front door as he called into the radio. I heard him mentioning everything Sydney told him about my so-called attack. One of the other officers continued talking to me, but his voice faded in my mind as all I could do was think of how I would make Mr. and Mrs. Bland pay for not giving me a chance at the life I wanted.

The officer returned from outside and beckoned for the brunette to step into the living room with him. Howard expressed concern.

"What's going on?" he asked.

The third officer spoke up. "Just give them a moment. I'm sure they'll be back in here to fill you in."

The officer was right. The other two came back in, and the brunette addressed me.

"Ms. Mills, I'm going to have to ask you again to leave."

"Why? You all just admitted that you can't make me leave."

"Well, you might want to leave anyway," the brunette said. "Your former apartment manager is looking for you and is planning to press charges for the damages you did to their property."

Sydney gasped. "She told us that the young man from the Madison did that."

The officer continued. "If he did, there was never a complaint made about vandalism or a rape. The only report we have is from the apartment management, stating she destroyed the apartment and caused thousands of dollars in damages."

Sydney and Howard looked at each other, seemingly floored.

"So, you schemed your way into our home," Howard growled. He turned to the officer. "Please—take her out of here."

"Ms. Mills, once again, it would be in your best interest to leave. Is there anything you want to take with you?"

I wanted to say, "Yes, my man." But I refrained. I shook my head.

The officer continued. "Ok. My advice to you is that whenever you want to pick up your things, call us to escort you. This way, we can monitor the situation and keep things peaceful."

I didn't respond. Instead, I turned and walked toward the front door. Oh, the Blands might've thought they won, but it wasn't over. I didn't leave my life in Chicago for nothing. Either I would have what I wanted, or I would die trying.

# Sydney

## 17

Although the police told us not to change the locks, we only agreed so Roxie would leave the house. Surely, they didn't think we were some brand-new fools to leave the same locks on the door, so Roxie could have access to our home again. We watched Roxie drive away, and then about fifteen minutes later, all the police cars were gone, too. Howard and I walked back into the house, looked at each other and completed each other's thoughts.

"What time does The Home Depot close?" we said in unison.

I pulled up the information on my cell phone. We still had a little more than an hour left before the store would close, so Howard agreed to run get new locks while I stayed to make sure Roxie didn't return. I called Teresa to let her know Howard and I were patching things up, and that I would be there to get Hailey by morning. I appreciate that she got Hailey back out of the house as quickly as she could when she saw our steaming faces. I could only hope Hailey didn't hear anything on their way into the house.

Once I got off the phone, I turned on the alarm then headed upstairs to get comfortable. I put on a pair of shorts and my favorite T-shirt from Montego Bay, Jamaica. I wanted to shower, but then thought better of it until Howard could make it back home. I jumped on top of our bed and reached for my purse to grab my cell. I decided to call Melanie to fill her in. I told her everything—leaving out the part about Roxie having an affair with Kevin. But she knew.

I felt like a horrible friend for knowing about Roxie and Kevin, but at the same time, I didn't want to hurt Melanie. She and Kevin had been through so much already, and if there would be any chance of them saving their marriage, me bringing more bad news wouldn't have helped. Melanie told me she found out when Roxie texted Kevin one night. I was unclear as to whether she found out before I did, but she told me she understood why I didn't bring the bad news to her. Though Melanie and Kevin were far from in love again, he was home and they   continued to work at their marriage.

She couldn't believe it when I told her everything that transpired after moving Roxie into my home. As I professed the twist of what seemed like a dramatic plot from a movie, I couldn't believe my own ears. Roxie had to be some kind of evil. *Who let's years go by, and then decides they want to reclaim a man who is somebody else's husband?* I wondered. *Satan's daughter,* was the only answer I could think of. I was in midsentence when I heard the rapid beeps of the security system going off. I waited to hear the three short beeps, signaling the alarm had been disarmed before making a move. I felt confident it was Howard as I heard what sounded like plastic store bags swishing. I relaxed and returned to my conversation with Melanie. But after a couple of minutes, Howard didn't come up the stairs, so I knew I needed to check things out.

"Melanie, let me call you back," I said and hung up before she could respond.

I slid off the bed and put on my slippers. I called out to Howard as I headed to the door. "Babe, is that you?" There was no response, but I could still hear the bags. "Babe," I called again. Still no answer.

I ran down the stairs so fast, I damned near fell on my ass as my slippers caused me to miss a couple of steps. I landed on my feet though, but once at the bottom, I glanced at the front door. It was closed, but unlocked. I hurried into the kitchen. Roxie stood, staring at me, calm, but clearly deranged.

"You a'ight? Sounds like you damned near broke your neck coming down those stairs," she said then continued taking groceries from the bags.

"Roxie, what the fuck are you doing back here?"

She smiled politely. "I told you this is my home, too."

"Didn't the police tell you not to come here without calling them first?"

She pulled a bottle of wine from a paper bag and set it on the island. "Puh-lease . . . as if I would listen to them. I mean, would you?"

"Yes, I would!"

She cocked her head to one side. "Really? Then, let me ask why did I observe Howard pulling into the parking lot of The Home Depot?"

"I don't know what you're talking about. I don't keep tabs on my husband."

I watched as she pulled two large steaks from one of the bags and then turn to preheat the oven. "Yeah, it's a good thing I went to the Sam's Club not far from there to get these steaks or else I might not have seen him." She pulled pans from the cabinets, and then grabbed my apron. "I knew I needed to hurry to Kroger for my other items and get back here before he made it home." She tied the apron. "Maybe he'll take his time, so I can have dinner ready when he gets here. Oh," she said abruptly then paused to place her hand on her chest. "I only bought dinner for two. My husband and I need some alone time to sort out some things, so I hope you understand."

"Roxie! If you don't get your delusional ass out of my house, I swear I'm going to make you wish you never met me."

She laughed. "If anybody's delusional it's you, Syd—Little Miss Thick'ums. You really think my Frankie is going to choose you over me? I know you've seen him salivating over my thin waist, fine body, and tight ass. He can't wait to taste this!"

I lunged at her, but unbeknownst to me, Roxie pulled a knife from the counter around the time she searched the cabinets for pans. Everything happened so quickly, I hardly knew I was stabbed. She caught me in the left shoulder as I charged her. Startled, I knocked the knife from the ball of my shoulder and blood poured down my arm like a waterfall. I clutched my shoulder, kicked out of my slippers then turned to run up the stairs. Howard entered the house through the kitchen door as Roxie was swift behind me. I heard things crashing to the floor as he dropped his bags and gave chase. I made it to my bedroom and turned to see Roxie and Howard tussling near the top of the stairs. He yelled for me to lock the bedroom door.

I did as I was told then looked around the room for my cell phone. It was still on the bed. I stumbled to it, dripping blood onto the comforter and dialed 9-1-1.

"9-1-1, do you need police, fire, or ambulance?" the dispatcher asked.

"I need police and ambulance!"

"What's your emergency?"

"We have an intruder. A woman is inside our home, fighting on the stairs with my husband."

"Is she armed?"

"Yes, she has a knife, and I've been stabbed!"

As the dispatcher typed, I could hear Roxie yelling something about making Howard pay for not choosing her.

"What's your name, ma'am?"

"Sydney Bland, and the woman who is fighting with my husband is Roxanne Mills. The police escorted her away from here earlier. She's not supposed to be back here."

Howard and Roxie were clearly struggling because they both panted and growled deeply, sounding like animals in distress as their bodies bumped into the walls.

"State your address, please," the dispatcher asked.

I rattled our address. Just as I finished, thunderous thuds of Howard and Roxie rolling down the steps made me drop the phone. I unlocked the bedroom door and peeped out. I couldn't see either of them, and they were dead silent.

"Howard, are you ok?" I yelled. He didn't answer.

I could hear the dispatcher calling for me. I dashed back into the room and picked up the phone.

"Tell the police to hurry, please!" I screamed.

"What's going on now, ma'am?" I heard her ask, but I didn't bother answering as I looked around for anything I could use to protect me and my husband.

My shoulder bled profusely, so I kept a tight grip on it as much as possible. As I headed out of the bedroom, I noticed large globs of my blood on the floor, the bedroom door and the walls as I exited the room. I went into the hall toward the stairs, calling out to Howard, but there was no response. On the way down the stairs, I could see Roxie and Howard at the bottom. They both lay out cold. I hurried to Howard, leaving bloody handprints on the wrought iron railing.

"Baby, are you ok?" I asked, kneeling beside him.

He groaned as he fought to fully regain consciousness. I wanted to pull him as far away from Roxie as possible, but my arm was too weak. I stood, trying to determine how to best scoot him. Suddenly, I felt a sharp gash across my leg, just above the ankle. Roxie was alert, and she wielded the knife, going for more blood. I hopped out of the way just as she swung the knife again, but this time, I landed on the floor.

I noticed Roxie was hurt. She attempted to stand, but she had trouble getting up. She moaned and held her side. She also screamed as she strained to lean on one of her forearms for support as she tried to get up.

I took the opportunity to scurry backwards as she struggled. I made it over to the console just before the kitchen entry and propped myself on it. I was winded and couldn't go any farther. I sat, panting, watching Roxie as she managed to get on her feet. The look in her eyes was unnerving—one that said nothing could stop her. She placed one foot in front of her, nearly toppling to the floor, but she used the wall to help her balance. As she took another step, Howard sat up and grabbed her leg.

Roxie was furious. Her scream was more like a roar as she lifted the knife high above her head, steadying it to land into Howard's back. But before she could lower it, the knife flung in midair.

BOOM. BOOM. BOOM. BOOM. BOOM.

Thank goodness I could still use my right hand to shoot. I managed to get my nine-millimeter from our bedroom before heading downstairs. I didn't know if I would have to use it, but I sure as hell wasn't scared.

Just a few minutes later, the police announced themselves as they entered our home. Roxie lay on the floor just under the stairs. Howard sat by my side, using a towel to apply pressure to my leg as I held on to my arm.

An EMT came in to resuscitate Roxie while another one attended to my wounds. After brief treatment, I was placed onto a gurney, headed to the hospital as I watched an EMT cover Roxie with a white sheet. I can't say I felt anything for the deceased woman who was already damaged beyond repair.

# Acknowledgements

To my loving husband: Mike, thank you for allowing me to be me. You believe in my dreams and support me without question. I love you so much for that.

Thank you to all of my readers for your love and continued support. You are the absolute best readership, and I mean that.

Thank you to all of my family and friends for always being there.

Thank you, Kay, for always having my back when I need your editorial eyes.

# Who Is Alisha Yvonne?

Playwright, Screenwriter, and National Bestselling Author, Alisha Yvonne is a native Memphian. She is the Essence® Bestselling Author of *Lovin' You Is Wrong* and *I Don't Wanna Be Right*. She is also nationally known for *Naughty Girls, Who's Fooling Who*, and her highly talked-about *The CleanUp Woman* series.

Look for her *Hopeland High* novels, *If I Were A Boy*, and *Soulja Girl*. She is currently working on her next release in the *The CleanUp Woman* series.

Write with Alisha Yvonne in on Facebook in her community for aspiring writers titled <u>My Page-Turner Unleashed: Aspiring Writers</u> or join her Facebook Community titled <u>Alisha Yvonne Readers</u>